Slocum's six-gun ̲ ̲ ̲ ̲ ̲ ̲ ̲ ̲ ̲ ̲ ̲ ̲ ̲ ̲ tightened. He
didn't care if this was a fair fight. The gunman had
tried to bushwhack him when he was unarmed. But
the man's speed was blinding. He drew and got off
a wild shot in Slocum's direction. Slocum squeezed
off his shot and felt the familiar recoil in his hand.
But there was no sense of hitting his target. Spinning
fast, Slocum came around the corner of the stable.
His Colt Navy was leveled and ready to fire. But the
gunfighter had vanished into thin air . . .

JAKE LOGAN

SLOCUM'S SILVER

J
JOVE BOOKS, NEW YORK

SLOCUM'S SILVER

A Jove Book / published by arrangement with
the author

PRINTING HISTORY
Jove edition / October 1995

All rights reserved.
Copyright © 1995 by Jove Publications, Inc.
This book may not be reproduced in whole
or in part, by mimeograph or any other means,
without permission. For information address:
The Berkley Publishing Group, 200 Madison Avenue,
New York, New York 10016.

ISBN: 0-515-11729-3

A JOVE BOOK®
Jove Books are published by The Berkley Publishing Group,
200 Madison Avenue, New York, New York 10016.
JOVE and the "J" design are trademarks
belonging to Jove Publications, Inc.

PRINTED IN THE UNITED STATES OF AMERICA

10 9 8 7 6 5 4 3 2 1

SLOCUM'S SILVER

1

"Fire in the hole!"

The cry echoed through the narrow valley and up the mountainside to John Slocum. He knelt down, arms over his head to protect himself from flying debris. Seconds later, the earth shook under his feet. He worried that Arly Penks had set too large a charge of giant powder in their mine. Slocum waited for the rain of sharp rock and the inevitable slow cascade of dust to fall before standing and brushing himself off.

"Everyone all right?" he shouted to his two partners. Slocum saw the slender Arly Penks wave warily, sending a new cloud of dust into the air with the movement. From behind their rundown mining shack came the taller, older, heavyset Happy Harry Harlan. As was his wont, a huge smile ran from ear to ear, showing his broken front tooth finished off in shining gold.

"Don't worry your pretty head none, Slocum," Harlan called. "That there little toot ain't gonna do in the likes of us. Not when we're settin' on top of the world, all fat and sassy and gettin' ready to be millionaires!"

Slocum made his way down the hillside, still brushing

the fine, choking dust out of his duds. Penks was the blaster, but Slocum knew a tad about the art and thought his partner had used too much black powder. The Silver Jackass Mine was a profitable hole in the side of the mountain, and he didn't want it caving in, blocking their road to a fortune in silver. The Comstock Lode had made dozens of men filthy rich. Slocum wanted to add his name to that list.

"We can't work the mine right away," Slocum said, eyeing the destruction wrought by the oversized charge. "The dust needs to settle. For quite a while."

"And I need something to settle the dust in my throat," agreed Happy Harry. He laughed in delight. "We been workin' up a storm. It's only fittin' we go into Virginia City and swallow a little of their tarantula juice!" He slapped Slocum on the back, causing a new dust storm. Nowhere was free of the cloaking dust, making Slocum agree with his partner about getting some liquor for his parched gullet. Slocum turned to see the balding, dark-fringed, clean-shaven Penks working his way down the rock-strewn mountainside.

For a moment, Slocum had the feeling he was watching a rat furtively making its way into a grain elevator. Then he shook off the notion. He didn't know much about Arly Penks, but Happy Harry thought well of him, and the hard-rock miner had been making a decent living for more years than Slocum had been around.

"We can't go into the mine for a spell," Penks said, unknowingly repeating what Happy Harry had already decided.

"Then it's into town. I'll buy you two gents a drink," Happy Harry declared, laughing at some unknown joke. "Then you can each buy me two!"

Slocum used his blue bandanna to wipe sweat and grime from his face. He could use a bath and shave, but he doubted that was what his two partners intended once they arrived in town. Virginia City had a saloon for every fifteen residents, or so it was rumored. Slocum had never ciphered it out, and it didn't much matter. B Street, the main street through the middle of town, was paved with crushed low-grade ore, which caused it to sparkle in the sunlight. That set the mood for the entire of Virginia City and the Comstock.

Uphill lay A Street, Howard Street, and Summit Street, where the first of the silver mines had been discovered. Even higher up on Mount Davidson shafts dropped a thousand feet into the solid rock. Some said as much as 750 miles of tunnels ran under Virginia City, but Slocum cared nothing about them. His sole interest lay in the Silver Jackass Mine and the silver ore the three of them pulled from it. The first of the Comstock claims, O'Reily and Mc-Laughlin's Ophir, had assayed at $4800 a ton in silver and $3200 in gold. Slocum had seen two different assays on the Silver Jackass, and both ran more than $6000 a ton in silver.

Every 2000 pounds of ore they dragged from the ground brought each of the three partners $2000. Slocum had worked as a cowboy on trail drives for $30 a month and grub. This was better.

"We can fetch some timbers from town," Penks said, scratching himself. "Then we can go drinking."

"Whatever suits you," Happy Harry agreed. "As long as there's some hard drinkin' wedged in there somewhere!" He went off to hitch up the jackass to their wagon.

Slocum asked Penks, "Was it necessary to use so much powder? That block of granite we hit was hard, but you might have brought down the mountain on us."

"I know what I'm doing," Penks said sharply. His bright blue eyes narrowed as he stared at Slocum, again giving the hint of a trapped rat. He had a long, snoutlike face and protruding nose hair bristled more like a rat's whiskers than anything approaching human. Slocum shook his head.

"Didn't mean anything by it. The more you blast, the harder we work to clean out the debris. And I surely do not want to see the roof come crashing down. That would cause us a month or more unneeded work.''

"You might have put up the money for this mine, Slocum, but you don't know squat about mining.'' Arly Penks swung around and stalked off. He didn't do too good a job of it, looking more foolish than menacing.

Slocum heaved a sigh. He had come into a pile of money when he found two stockholders of the Consolidated Virginia Company that didn't know odds at poker. Rather than parlaying his poke into a bigger one, Slocum had decided to join them in pulling ore from the ground. Happy Harry had needed a few dollars to begin work on the Silver Jackass. The field assay looked promising, and Slocum had poured the whole thousand dollars into the venture. Arly Penks had joined them when it became apparent that two men would never be able to drive into the hard rock and get more than aching backs from the effort. Even with three, the work was arduous.

It was also profitable. Slocum pushed his dislike of Penks from his mind when he reminded himself he had recouped his money—and more—in the first month they had worked the mine.

"Jump on up, Slocum, or we'll be leavin' you behind for certain. I've got such a powerful thirst nothin's standin' in my way!'' Happy Harry Harlan motioned for Slocum to jump into the rear of their wagon. Slocum did so, glad that Penks sat on the hard wagon seat with Happy Harry. Slocum stretched out on some burlap bags, wedged himself between sacks of ore being taken in to the smelter, and tried to sleep. The bouncing wagon and sharp points of ore poking into him made sleep difficult, but when Slocum shook himself awake, they were driving down B Street and Harry was chortling about finding just the right drinking emporium.

"That's the one we try this time, gents,'' he said. "We can handle the ore delivery later.''

Slocum didn't cotton much to leaving their precious

cargo in the wagon with no one to watch over it, but the tickle in his throat now matched that of Harlan's. Penks followed them at a distance, as if wary of being seen in their company. How Harry chose from the dozens of saloons was something that Slocum couldn't figure out. They went past the Howling Wilderness, the Old Washoe Club, and even the Sawdust Corner in favor of the Silver Sunbeam.

"Two of your worst," Happy Harry called to the barkeep. He paused a moment, took note of Penks, then added, "and another one for my fine partner, Arly Penks!"

Slocum swallowed the fiery liquor and let it wash away the aches and dust and memories he had accumulated. The whiskey settled in his belly and burned quietly. He nodded when the barkeep tapped the bottle, silently asking if he wanted another.

Slocum had barely lifted the shot glass to his lips when he froze. From outside came the loud clanging of a bell and frantic shouts. It might have been the worst of all possible sounds.

"Fire!" came the cry. "There's a fire uphill and its going down below!"

"Now don't that beat all," Happy Harry said, staring at his second drink. He quickly finished it. "Jist when I'm settlin' in for serious drunkenness, somethin' interrupts me."

Slocum followed suit and downed his drink. He had the feeling he was going to need the liquid fortification the firewater gave. A blaze aboveground in Virginia City was deadly. The buildings sprouted like so many mushrooms—tinder-dry mushrooms that would explode into fierce flame, should even a spark touch them. Too many people had come to the Comstock too fast for anyone to worry over anything.

But a fire going underground, down in a mine, was even worse.

The mines were suffocatingly hot deep under the earth's

surface, and streams of 170-degree water sometimes gushed forth with scalding effect. But what Slocum feared most lay trapped in pockets within the hard rock. Gas. The fire might chew on the dry timbers and find a natural gas pocket that could explode with enough force to blow the top off the mountain.

It would take more than a miracle to save anyone trapped down in the mine if the gas detonated. In a way, Slocum thought, that might be the best way to go. Fast.

He shuddered as he and dozens of other men hurried along Virginia City's streets toward the clanging bell at the headquarters of the Monumental Engine Company No. 6 up on the divide between Virginia City and Gold Hill. Already the fire engine was being pulled out, and its team made ready for the arduous trip uphill.

"We're goin' for first water!" shouted one red-shirted fireman, struggling to pull the heavy engine. No mule would pull the engine up such a steep slope; twenty men did. Slocum and Happy Harry lent a hand and kept the engine moving. It took more than ten minutes to reach the site of the fire. Smoke billowed from the shaft. The wooden headframe was already gone.

"Glad to see so many of you," called the fire captain. "Get on to the hose trucks, men. We need all the hose we can get. The fire's down in the Croaking Frog, and it's likely to be a hard one to extinguish." He cupped his mouth and shouted, "Man the brakes! Get to pumping! We're here first. We've got first water!"

"First water!" the cry went up as the men started pumping hard to get water spewing from their engine. Slocum understood the pride the men took in being first to the fire, first to put water on the blaze, and maybe first to die. Becoming a fireman in Virginia City required considerable courage and skill, and not everyone who volunteered was accepted. Every company had to vote on recruits and five blackballs sent the volunteer on his way.

Slocum stood back and watched the men work. This

might be a vicious fire to put out. The Croaking Frog Mine was one of the few independents left along the divide. The others were owned by the Virginia Consolidated and the California Consolidated companies. That meant the timbers would be spaced farther apart and were possibly older and of inferior quality. The fire could ruin the mine for all time if the roof collapsed.

Then he heard shouts from higher on the hillside that chilled him even more.

"Cap'n, we got men trapped. Three, maybe more."

"We got a night's work ahead of us," Happy Harry said, the smile finally gone from his lips. "And here I had my heart set on nothin' more than polishin' off a bottle of Old Overholt." Harry Harlan hitched up his canvas trousers and set off. Slocum trailed close behind. Around them rattled the engine and hose trucks and hundreds of men flocking from all over Virginia City. Two other engine companies, the Knickerbocker No. 5 and Young America Engine Company No. 2, rattled up to join the fight. He couldn't help noticing that Arly Penks was not among the newcomers. Slocum shook his head. When trouble reared its head, miners had to pull together. Why Penks refused to join in was his business, but Slocum didn't like it much. It showed a weakness of character that rankled.

Then Slocum forgot everything about the failings of his partner. The smoke billowing from cracks in the ground showed the extent of the blaze. Timbers had already caught fire and threatened the integrity of the mine itself.

"Here, gents, put these on. It helps us keep track of you when things get real confusing." Slocum took a wide-brimmed, thickly padded brown leather helmet that fit too snugly and a bright red canvas shirt that hung on him like a curtain. Still, the helmet would keep falling rocks from doing too much damage to his skull if he got into the mine, and through the gathering pall of heavy black smoke, anyone wearing a red jacket was more easily spotted.

"Help, we need some help!" called a fireman from the

hose truck. Seeing there was nothing he could do to help those working the engine, Slocum began dragging lengths of the heavy hose off the truck. He knew the hose would get a lot heavier once water started flowing through it. He found himself working shoulder to shoulder with Happy Harry, who hummed to himself as he worked.

"Harry," grunted Slocum, "why are you always so damned happy?"

For an answer he received a guffaw. "Why, Slocum, it's like this. You can laugh or you can cry. Me, I prefer to enjoy what life has to offer and not to cry over spilt milk."

"That how you got your nickname?" Slocum struggled to drag the length of hose along the ground. He felt the rock beneath his boots heating from the fire raging below. Anyone in the Croaking Frog Mine was a goner by now. They had to be. He hoped the volunteers would be able to cool off the rock and arrest the spread before it took out the entire mine or found gas.

"Hell, no, Slocum, that's not why I took to callin' myself Happy Harry. Not at all. Harry Harlan, that's what my ma named me when I was born. But the other kids took to callin' me Harhar. You know how cruel kids can be. I figgered Happy Harry was better, and it seemed to please the others, to boot."

He rocked back and let his boisterous good nature spill forth. Slocum had to admit a liking for the man. Nothing dampened his spirits.

"Hook the hose to the engine," ordered the fire captain. "We're ready to get to serious pumping." He pointed vaguely at the line running down the hill. They had to pump water up more than a quarter mile from a reservoir.

"How'd the fire start?" Slocum wasn't sure it mattered, but curiosity burned as brightly in him as the fire below his feet.

"Can't say, but we're afraid they were two-jacking and hit a pocket of gas. One spark of steel moving across rock, and that'd be all she wrote."

Slocum staggered slightly. For a moment, he thought his knees had turned rubbery on him. Then he realized the ground shook. More explosions tore at the troubled mine.

"Where are the men? Are they goners?" Slocum finished the connection and shouted over the loud clanking of the engine.

"That machine will throw a stream of water a hundred seventy-five feet, and that's after it goes down a hundred feet of hose," the captain said, "and it ain't worth a bucket of warm spit. Not when the fire's underground. The best we can hope for is to keep the fire from bustin' out and catching in the weeds." He kicked at the dry brush on the mountainside. He cinched the broad belt tighter around his waist, making sure the black leather was held firmly by the huge silver buckle showing his rank and fire company. Then he rushed off to order the engine crew to spray down the rock in an effort to keep everything from combusting around them.

"Ain't no good," Happy Harry said.

"What?" Slocum stared into the mouth of the mine where smoke came out in choking clouds.

"The fancy-ass engine of theirs. Might be useful if Virginia City itself caught fire. It would work wonders on wood buildings. There's nothin' to aim the water at with an underground fire."

"Not unless you dragged the hose into the mine," Slocum finished. They stared at each other a moment. Slocum knew this was the height of folly. If he wanted to kill himself, he could think of a dozen better ways.

He and Happy Harry never hesitated as they hefted the hose with its one-inch brass nozzle and turned the spray full onto the mouth of the mine. Together, they started dragging it forward, into the curtains of heat gusting from the Croaking Frog.

"Hey, there, don't get any closer. That's dangerous!" yelled the fire captain.

"You said there was men in the mine, didn't you, cap'n?"

"We know of at least three, maybe two more. But you can't go down there. It's too dangerous. You have to spray the water around and—"

"Keep the water pumping," Slocum ordered. He hunched his shoulders, tugged harder, and got the hose slithering along the rocky ground behind him like a slippery inch-thick snake. The heat threatened to blister his face as he and Harry Harlan moved closer to the mouth of the mine, but the spray cooled off the rock, killed some of the blistering heat, and got them into the mine itself.

Slocum would have backed away, giving up those inside as lost, but he thought he heard distant cries for help.

He and Happy Harry exchanged a final look of determination, then jerked hard on the hose to get some slack before plunging into the choking, blinding inferno.

2

Slocum glanced through the thick smoke at red-shirted Harry Harlan. For once, the smile had vanished from the man's face and a grim expression reflected the strain of dragging the heavy, kicking fire hose. But the front gold tooth shone like a beacon through the gloom and made Slocum smile.

"Let's get in there," Slocum said, coughing. To his surprise, Harry held back.

"Your bandanna, Slocum. Wet it from the hose and tie it over your mouth and nose," Happy Harry called. The roar of the fire deeper in the mine was as much a physical assault on Slocum as the blasts of scorching heat and smoke gushing outward, but he realized this small ploy might save them once they got deeper into the mine. He quickly obeyed, even as Happy Harry pulled off part of his shirt-sleeve and thrust it into the harsh flow of water from the nozzle.

Behind, from the area around the pump, Slocum heard loud shouts. Someone wanted to cut off the water to force them to retreat, but the fire captain's good sense prevented this. The water kept flowing, and Slocum counted this as saving their lives.

A sudden gas eruption from deep in the bowels of the mine sent out a fiery messenger. Tongues of flame sought his body even as sharp needles dug into his face and hands. He opened the nozzle and erected a curtain of water to protect them. The water sizzled and hissed as it vaporized, but the torrents of heat cooled enough to keep from frying them like Sunday morning sausage.

Through it all, Slocum heard faint cries of men begging for help.

"Where?" he called to his partner. "I can't see past the end of my arm in this smoke." Slocum savagely twisted the nozzle to get a finer mist spraying forth, but the adjustment failed. He got a deluge of water that proved almost uncontrollable. Like some serpent come to life, the hose bucked and kicked at him, trying to slip wetly from his grasp.

Slocum leaned for a moment against one hot wall to pull his boot from the muck forming on the floor. Too much water had accumulated for easy walking. The dirt and debris from the explosion and mining had turned to sucking mud that threatened to trip him up with every step. To get his bearings, he turned off the water. The snake-hose went to sleep in his grip but remained as rigid as a steel rod.

"I seem to remember a fork in the shaft. The new drift goes toward the worst of the fire," Happy Harry said, squinting against the smoke. "Keep movin' to your left."

Slocum opened the nozzle again and sprayed down the timbers, charred and smoldering from the intense heat. He noted how only the backside of the timbers, the part toward the fire, had turned to charcoal. A first hot wave had come from the depths, then only smoke followed. That single explosion might have trapped men, but without continuing gas eruptions, they might be safe.

Somehow, in the snapping teeth of the smoke and heat, Slocum wondered how that might be possible. He wiped at his tear-filled eyes and felt grit on his cheeks. His lips chapped and his flesh stung from tiny cinders flying through the mine. But he kept moving forward until he found the left-hand tunnel. It was unscathed by fire or blast, but the vibration had caused parts of the roof to collapse, blocking entrance or exit. Spraying everywhere to cool off the rock, he inched forward until he came to the end of the canvas hose. No amount of tugging would budge its balky length.

"We've run to the end. They can't give us no more," Happy Harry shouted. "You see anybody ahead?"

"I can hear them," Slocum said, putting his hand against the plug of rock barring his way. A gentle vibration showed that someone still lived and tapped out a doleful signal for would-be rescuers. He moved back to the fork in the tunnel. From downhill in this sloping shaft came the worst of the smoke. He forced the brass nozzle between sagging timber and hard-rock wall and left it spraying a constant plume of water. The water would hold back the choking smoke and give a few minutes of protection for what Slocum knew had to be done.

"Got a pick," said Harry, who had already arrived at the same conclusion. "There's a shovel. Let's get to high-gradin' their mine!" The portly man chuckled and set off to swing the pick against the fall of rock blocking the left-hand tunnel. He worked with a vengeance, iron crashing into rock and sending fat blue sparks flying into the darkness. Slocum found himself hard-pressed to muck away the pieces his partner produced off the rockfall. Shoulder muscles knotting and back aching, Slocum kept moving stone away until he stood knee deep in rubble.

At the top of the fall he saw the flash of light—weak, faint, and unsteady, but definitely light. Forcing his shovel into the tiny hole, he widened it until he could poke his head through. On the other side of the collapsed tunnel, he saw three men huddled together, a single carbide lamp sputtering bravely on the stony floor.

Slocum bumped his head and thanked his lucky stars for

the fireman's leather helmet as he wiggled through the hole. For a moment he thought the men were dead, possibly suffocated in an airtight pocket. They sat unmoving. Then one turned his head slowly toward Slocum.

"They made it. They made it through!" shouted the miner. The other two were even slower to respond. One dropped a rock hammer he had been using to send the steady message of need. The clangor as it landed startled Slocum.

"You hurt bad?" Slocum asked, moving to the man's side. He saw one man could do little more than blink his eyes. From the blood on his chest, he might have been crushed by falling rock. There might be no way of moving him with a busted rib cage that wouldn't kill him outright. The other man favored a leg. White bone gleamed in the faint light; Slocum knew a compound fracture when he saw one.

"I dug all I could, but I reached the end," the one miner in good condition said. "Truth to tell, I lost my way and didn't know which way was toward the surface."

Slocum understood how a man could get disoriented underground. Worse, he saw how the miners had worked Croaking Frog. They followed veins of ore haphazardly, wandering up and down and around like some drunken subterranean snake instead of systematically exploiting their claim.

"Harry can help you out," Slocum said to the man with the broken leg. "Don't waste time in the tunnel. Get out as quick as you can."

"Like a rabbit," the miner promised. He tried to smile, but the pain erased it quickly. Slocum knew he hurt the man terribly shoving him through the tiny hole they had dug for the rescue, but he didn't care. The roar from the other fork in the mine grew louder. Maybe the fire had found a stack of timbers destined for new tunneling, or perhaps it had hit more gas. Whatever fed it, the fire was getting worse, and he was getting itchy to get out.

"How are we going to get Bob Ed out?"

Bob Ed had to be the miner with the crushed chest. Slocum knew only one way, and it might kill the man. He turned his back to the supine miner and motioned for the other to hoist him up. Slocum staggered under the weight for a moment, then bent forward and made his way to the hole, the miner's arms tightly clasped around his neck.

"I owe you a drink, Bob Ed. Don't you go and die on me till I buy it for you," the other miner said. Slocum let the man do the talking to keep the injured miner distracted and fighting for his life. If he ever gave in to the pain he must feel, he would die.

Stumbling down the rocky slope on the far side of the hole, Slocum bent almost double and walked toward the fork. The fire still raged unabated below them. He considered leaving the hose, then knew it was costly and would be needed in other fires. He took the time to close the nozzle and pull it free from its berth. Then he followed the other miner from the Croaking Frog. The firemen outside could pull the hose free once all the miners were safe.

Slocum stumbled along for what seemed an hour, the weight on his back breaking him down a bit more with each step. He knew now how the old cavalry mounts felt after five years in service. If he got out alive, he would be swaybacked for the rest of his life. And then he had the sensation of being away from the hot rock tomb all around him. Cool wind blew into his face, clean, pure air laced with a hint of pine from far off and from the dry sage under his feet. He straightened and went cold inside.

Slocum thought he had gone blind. Then he realized the sun had set. It was night. He and Happy Harry had been working in the mine far longer than he had thought possible, considering the hellish conditions there. He blinked and tried to wipe sweat away from his face, getting tangled in the bandanna still around his mouth and nose. Slocum jumped a foot when the cheer went up from the assembled firemen.

"Get Doc Hanley," someone said. Another helped Bob Ed lie flat on the ground and another slapped Slocum on the back so hard he almost toppled over. Life crowded in on him from every direction. He had been boxed in, rock walls just inches in any direction—and hot rock, at that. The air had been deadly, and he had rushed into a world filled only with his own efforts to get the miners to safety.

Now he was safe and in the open. He wiped his eyes again and saw the Big Dipper. Never had a set of stars looked more appealing to him. Never.

"Give him air. There's nothing in that there mine shaft to breathe 'cept smoke." Slocum immediately recognized Happy Harry's loud voice and silently thanked his partner for pushing back the onlookers.

He stumbled away from the heat boiling at his back, then some distance from the Croaking Frog Mine, he sat cross-legged on the ground, trying to get his wits about him. The doctor was already at work on the rib-crashed miner while two volunteer firemen set the second miner's broken leg. The third miner argued with the fire captain over the best way to put out the blaze in the mine.

"Snuff it out now, I say," the miner declared. "A single charge right at the fork will do it."

"Might have an underground fire that would burn forever. Can't have it getting under the town. All Virginia City might go up when we least expect it."

The miner shook his head. "I was a coal miner in Virginny 'fore I came out to the Comstock. There's no seam running through the Frog that will smolder. If we cut off the air, it'll snuff the fire. I know a blast can do it. Cuts off all the air for just a second and that puts out the fire slick as snot on glass."

Reluctantly, the fire captain went along with the miner's scheme. The pair of them vanished into the mouth of the Croaking Frog Mine with a small bundle of dynamite. The explosion a few seconds after they ran back out shook the ground. And then came a deathly silence that caused Slocum to worry that he had gone deaf.

He realized about the same time as the others that the roaring fire had been stilled. The ground was still fiercely hot and would take days to cool off, but the heart of the fire had been quelled. The blast had worked as the miner claimed it would.

The miner brushed himself off, said a few words to the fire captain, then walked over to stand above Slocum, blotting out the precious stars and cool breeze blowing off the Sierras.

"They tell me your name's Slocum. Let me shake your hand for what you done. That was about the bravest thing I ever seen." The grizzled miner Slocum had rescued shoved out a thick, dirty paw. They shook, the man's powerful grip hard and sincere.

"How're your partners?"

"Bob Ed's gonna be jist fine. The doc says he can patch him up good as new in a week or two. A couple busted ribs, but his lungs are still blowin'. And McDermont's already hobbling around. We're gonna have to call him Gimpy from now on, I reckon." The miner laughed at this. "My name's Blasko, and I owe you a drink. Hell, I owe you my life!"

Slocum got to his feet and looked around. The Monumental Engine Company worked at their hoses to spray down the ground, hoping to find cracks leading into the now blocked section of the Croaking Frog. If they could force water directly underground, they could eliminate all chance that the fire would spring back to life.

"The entire stope we been workin' is gone. The dynamite the cap'n and me planted took care of it, but that's all right, since it got that hungry bastard of a fire, too. You and your partner saved us, and we can work to get the mine back open. Beats hell out of the Croaking Frog being our grave."

Happy Harry joined them and the trio returned to the saloon where they had started their drinking binge. A few onlookers joined the small parade and soon they had half of Virginia City trailing behind. Two men rushed onward to open the swinging doors for Slocum and Happy Harry, and Blasko shoved one man back when he tried to follow them too closely. Inside, Slocum saw Arly Penks at the rear of the long, narrow room, nursing a drink. The expression on his face was a mixture of surprise and awe that they had returned—or maybe that they had come back looking like something the cat dragged in.

"What happened to you?" Penks asked.

This set Blasko off on a long, loud recitation of everything that had occurred: how the gas pocket exploded, how the three miners had tried to escape, only to go down the wrong tunnel in their confusion, how the roof had collapsed, and the miners' subsequent injuries, then the tale of how Slocum and Happy Harry had rescued them like angels swooping down from some cloudy section of heaven.

"They're my partners," Penks said, moving closer. "You picked a pair of good men, and it is my pleasure to buy you gents a bottle each."

Slocum saw how Penks tried to get into the circle but was kept at bay by the firemen now crowding into the saloon, each wanting to talk to the heroes. Then came the newspaper reporters from the *Territorial Enterprise* and the *Gold Hill News*. They wanted every detail of the fire and rescue. Slocum was glad to let Harry do the talking. And when Happy Harry faltered, Blasko picked up smoothly.

Slocum wanted nothing more of the adulation he received. His body was blistered and aching, and all he wanted was a bath and good night's sleep. But he straightened when he heard Blasko's bull-throated bellow for silence.

"Hush up, you loudmouthed sons of bucks," Blasko shouted. "I got somethin' to say."

"Hell, Blasko, that's all you been doing since Slocum and Harry pulled your sorry ass out of the mine," another miner called. "I say we put you back into the Croaking

Frog so we can get some peace and quiet!''

This produced a round of laughter that died quickly when Blasko held up his hand.

"Let me say this while those no-account reporters are still sober.'' He cleared his throat and said, "Me and my partners got a real good claim in the Frog. We're pulling out better than eight thousand ounces of silver a month.''

Slocum was impressed. That meant the Croaking Frog was half again as good as the Silver Jackass—so far.

"I'm not much for these things, but I want to post a reward to the two men what saved us, Bob Ed Briggs, Mike McDermont, and Lew Blasko. I'm going to give them each one hundred ounces of silver!''

At this a cry went up. Slocum blinked at the generosity. He would have been content with receiving only the bottle of rotgut for his services. More than once he had gotten nothing but bullets aimed in his direction when he had tried to do a good deed.

After the third cheer died down, Slocum called for silence.

"Hey, Slocum, what you gonna do with the bullion?'' shouted a reporter, spitting on his pencil and ready to write down the words. Slocum paused when he saw how the reporter hung on his every word.

"I don't want to take Blasko's silver,'' Slocum said. A deathly hush fell. This was as bad as if he had called the miner a coward. No one refused what was freely given. Slocum hurried on to explain. "I want him to give the money to the Monumental Engine Company for more equipment. That way, we all share in Blasko's good nature.''

"Mine, too,'' shouted Happy Harry Harlan. "I'll toss my reward in with Slocum's. The Monumental Engine Company firemen are a good bunch of men, and they can use the silver to buy new hoses and maybe get a shirt that fits a proper-sized gent!'' Happy Harry stepped from the bar and showed how tightly the red canvas shirt stretched across his broad shoulders.

This got another round of laughter and cheering from the crowd.

Slocum fell back, letting Happy Harry bask in the crowd's approval for a while. But from behind he heard Arly Penks muttering angrily to himself, "Stupid sons of bitches. Two hundred ounces! And they throw it away!"

Slocum's other partner left the saloon, shaking his head.

3

"Yes, sir, Slocum, we coulda been rich. We coulda been spendin' up a storm back there in Virginia City, laughin' as the Washoe Zephyrs blew past us. You know that it's a fact there are saloons I've never been inside there in Virginia. Imagine that." Happy Harry Harlan shook his head as he honed the edge of the pickax. He held it up so the sun shone brightly off the part needed to penetrate some of the rockfall in the Silver Jackass Mine.

"We'll be rich from ore dug from our own mine," Slocum said. He dropped the burlap water bags with a wet squishing sound. One had developed a hole in it, which he had patched. The other needed filling at their sweet water well a hundred yards away at the bottom of the hill. All morning long Slocum had been toiling alongside Happy Harry to get their tools ready for the hard work of opening the new passage blown in their mine.

Slocum glanced around to find Arly Penks but didn't see the man. He pushed aside a smoldering anger at his partner. Happy Harry pulled his own load, but Penks was a horse of a different color. He had misjudged the amount of powder needed to blow the rock plugging their shaft and had

21

created many days of extra work. And now he had high-tailed it for parts unknown.

"There, on the mountain. See? Up high." Slocum squinted and pulled the edge of his broad-brimmed black Stetson down to shield his eyes. He saw something moving up there, something reflecting light off bright silver.

"Looks to be Penks," Happy Harry said, his eyes sharper than Slocum's. "Or maybe not. Cain't rightly tell who it is stirrin' up there." For once his humor turned sour. "I never saw a lazier man in all my born days than that Arly Penks. But if that's Arly, who's that palavering with him?"

"There's somebody else up there?" Slocum squinted a little harder but saw no one. The flash of silver vanished, leaving behind only a dark brown dot that might be Penks. As he watched, the man made his way downhill and details became sharper.

"It is Penks. But I don't know if he was talking to someone or hiding something," Slocum said. He tried to remember if they had any bullion in their camp. He didn't think so. The last load of ore had gone to the smelter, and when it came out of the stamping mill in ingot form, they would deposit it in the Virginia City Bank. For the first time in longer than he could remember, Slocum could buy equipment and food at a store and not have to worry about payment.

All he had to do was sign a draft against their deposit. But what if Penks kept some of the silver from reaching the bank and hid it? Slocum spat. Not trusting his own partner was a feeling he could do without. Working a mine was dangerous, and he had to rely on the others for his very life—and they had to rely on him.

The slightest hesitation might mean death. Right now, Slocum wasn't sure if he could rush out to save Arly Penks without ever thinking about it.

"If we don't see some sweat on his brow soon," Happy

Harry went on, "I'm for buying him out and workin' the claim on our own."

Slocum grunted as he hefted the water bags. He caught a shovel Happy Harry tossed him and then started for the mouth of the Silver Jackass. Debris trailed out from the blasting the day before, but the dust had finally settled. Slocum considered getting a hose from one of the volunteer fire companies and spraying into the mine. Getting the last of the dust from the air would improve his work and keep him from coughing half to death.

"Come on in, Slocum," urged Happy Harry. "I don't know if he intended to do it, but Penks done good. The granite plug is entirely gone, and you've got to see what was hidin' behind it."

Slocum stopped just inside the mine mouth and carefully lit a candle. Cupping his hand in front of it, he made his way deeper into the darkness. A few yards brought him to the rubble on the floor. Stumbling over it, he pushed to Happy Harry's side. The huge cork of rock they had encountered had shattered, and beyond it gleamed riches beyond Slocum's wildest dreams.

"Black sand?" He knelt and studied the fine grains on the floor under the dark vein running into the hillside.

"We used to call it bogus gold, back in the days 'fore we knew better," Happy Harry said. "I need to test it, but I got my suspicions—and they're all real good, Slocum. *Real good.*"

Happy Harry scraped along the exposed lode and collected more than a double handful of the black, grainy mineral. Slocum led the way to the mouth of the mine. For a moment, he thought he would find Arly Penks waiting for them, ready to get to work, but their partner was nowhere to be seen.

Slocum shrugged it off. He was more intent on watching Happy Harry do a field assay.

Taking his equipment from a canvas bag, the miner spread the tools of his trade around him in a fan-shaped array. Working with sureness of long practice, Happy Harry scraped some of the black mineral into a spoon, dried it over an alcohol lamp, and then carefully tapped the dry grains into a hollowed-out block of charcoal.

"What's happening?" Slocum asked, peering at the mass as it melted in Happy Harry's blowpipe. "I see a tiny bead of silver forming."

"Good news. If we had iron or nickel left after we got rid of the sulfates, there would be only a brown or red smear left."

"Might be lead," observed Slocum.

Happy Harry nodded as he worked with the tiny bead. "If it is, it will melt real fast again." He tapped the charcoal block to get the silver button to one side. It took several seconds of intense heat from the blowpipe before it melted.

Happy Harry looked up at Slocum. His eyes danced and the ever-present smile broadened to a face-stretching grin.

"Silver glance. That's what we started with, Slocum. Some sulfuret of silver that burns off real quick. No chlorides, no carbonates. This might assay out to an ounce a shovelful. A thousand ounces in every thousand of ore! Pure silver!"

Happy Harry started dancing about like a crazy man, waving his arms as if he might take to the air and fly away. Slocum sagged back, leaning against the side of the mountain that was going to make him a rich man. The reward from the miners in the Croaking Frog Mine had been generous, but now Slocum and Happy Harry Harlan would be able to buy and sell them a hundred times over.

If he felt generous enough, he could buy a steam pumper for every fire company in Virginia City *and* Gold Hill.

He had always dreamed of hitting it rich. Now he had, and he wasn't sure how he felt.

"Harry, what do we do about Penks? Do we offer to buy him out and not tell him about this?"

"That would be dishonest, Slocum. You know we have

to tell the ornery son of a buck.'' Happy Harry spoke the words, but his tone relayed his true feelings. "He did blow the lode open for us."

"But we're doing all the work. Where is he? We spotted him on the top of the hill, and then he vanished. He's never around when it comes to doing the real work."

"We mighta blasted without him. You said you had some experience," Happy Harry muttered.

"I would never have used that much giant powder. We might have missed the lode if I'd been blasting." Slocum wasn't sure how he felt about letting their slacker of a partner know what they had found.

"The lode might come to the surface somewhere else. We coulda found it that way and followed it into the hill," Harry said. "There's a thousand ways we mighta found the sulfuret."

"Let's get some of that ore out and think on it," Slocum said. "If he turns up, we can discuss the matter."

"I'm chompin' at the bit," Happy Harry said, his good humor returning. He took a long draft of water from the burlap bag Slocum had hung at the mouth of the mine, then plunged inside. Slocum followed closely, again carefully shielding the flame on his candle. At the rockfall, they began work in earnest. Happy Harry picked away the ore and Slocum lugged it to the mouth of the mine. When only powder remained on the floor, the two of them shoveled it into burlap bags so none of the sulfuret would be lost.

They might gain a dozen ounces of silver in each heavy bag of black dust.

All afternoon they worked, seldom resting in their rush to become rich. Just before sundown, Happy Harry halted and waved to Slocum to join him in the narrowest section of the mine shaft.

"We got problems again, Slocum. The lode veers off, away from the area opened by the blast. We played out quick."

"Another blast might open in this direction," Slocum

said, resting his hand against the rock keeping them from untold wealth.

"Can you do it?"

Before Slocum could answer, Arly Penks spoke up from behind. Both men jumped, not knowing their partner was listening.

"I can open it. I went into town to get more powder. What did you two find while I was gone?"

"Can't rightly say," Happy Harry lied without hesitation. His dishonesty startled Slocum, who thought it would be his cheerful partner who insisted on complete admission of their discovery. "We need some more work to be certain."

"Silver glance?" Penks rubbed the grainy sand between his fingers. "Might be a real find."

"Might be," Slocum allowed. "You said you went into town? Why didn't you let us know?"

"You're not my ma. I don't have to tell you my every move. Do you want me to blast here or not?"

"Blow it," Slocum said without hesitation. He had toiled all day and was ready to work all night.

The lure of silver did that to a man.

"Get on out of the shaft, then," Penks said. "Let me see how this is best set. And lug in those kegs of powder, will you? They're down at the shack."

Slocum and Happy Harry left their partner in the mine. They walked in silence for a few yards before Slocum spoke. "What do you think? Do we tell him what we took from the mine all day?"

"Blast first, talk later," Happy Harry decided. "I'm not up to cheatin' any man, especially a partner, but I ain't inclined to let any man cheat me, neither. And Penks ain't been doin' squat."

Slocum nodded. He felt much the same way. Penks cheated them out of a decent day's work whenever he wandered off, whether he went into Virginia City or traipsed up the side of the mountain to meet with somebody. How much he ought to get from the mine was a matter they had to resolve soon.

"You bring the miner's black fuse?" Penks asked in his peevish tone. "I need fresh fuse, not the old rat's tail you had laying around in the shack."

"It burned a timed foot every minute," Slocum said. There had been nothing wrong with the old fuse they had stocked up on. It had been sold at bargain prices because some prospector who had gone bust traded it for food to get on to another mountain in some other county, not because it was defective.

Penks snorted in contempt at Slocum's opinion. He reeled off three feet of the new fuse and bit it with his back teeth. Penks spat a length of the black cord to the ground and then shoved it into the keg of black powder. He hefted it and vanished into the mine.

"Need any help?" Slocum shouted after him.

"Stay out, Slocum. Don't want you getting yourself hurt 'cause you don't know what you're doing."

"A particularly disagreeable gent," Happy Harry said in a level voice. Slocum read the decision on his partner's face. Unless Penks was more clever than they thought, he would never know what they had found and the two of them would buy him out for a song and a dance—and to hell with ethics. Arly Penks had done nothing to earn his share.

"You got it braced against the right wall, Penks?" He cupped his hands around his mouth and shouted again when he got no answer.

"Yeah, yeah, everything's goin' just fine," came Penk's reply. The small man ducked from the mine and shooed them away.

"Fire in the hole!" he called.

Slocum and Happy Harry scrambled down the hill for the protection offered by their miner's shack. Slocum counted slowly, but after three minutes passed and no explosion rocked the ground, he looked up.

"What happened, Penks?"

"Maybe I used your fuse instead of the good stuff," Penks said, frowning. "I better go check to be sure the fuse didn't fizzle out."

"Let it rest for a few more minutes," suggested Happy Harry. "If the fuse wasn't timed proper, it might be burnin' slow. You don't want to walk into the middle of an explosion."

"I know what I'm doing," Penks said angrily. "You listen up, in case I need help."

Slocum and Happy Harry watched the smaller man hurry up the slope and pause at the mouth of the mine. Then he ducked inside.

"Gettin' dark. We ought to wait till morning to do this," Happy Harry said.

Slocum would have agreed except for the amount of dust raised. He didn't want to lose another day waiting for the air to clear before digging in the black sand that would make him rich.

"If we blast now, the dust will have settled by morning. Here, take a swig of water." Slocum turned and hefted one burlap bag, took a drink, and passed it to his partner. As Happy Harry drank, Slocum turned back to the mouth of the mine and frowned.

"What's taking him so long?" Slocum wondered aloud.

"Can't say. Setting a new fuse couldn't take this long, 'less something' bad is wrong."

Happy Harry took another drink and put down the bag when Penks's voice echoed down the twilight-cloaked hill.

"Slocum, Harlan, help! I can't, I don't, *help!*" The stark fear in Penks's cry froze Slocum for a moment. What had the man run afoul of in the mine?

Slocum and Happy Harry exchanged worried glances, then both lit out like scalded dogs, heading up the hillside. Slocum couldn't figure out what might have gone wrong, but it could mean the destruction of the Silver Jackass. He had won and lost fortunes, but he wasn't going to lose this one, not after all the hard work he had put into the mine.

"Where are you, Penks?" Slocum slid to a halt at the mouth of the mine. He heard nothing from inside. "Penks!"

"The candle, Slocum, get the candle," Happy Harry said.

Slocum took down the burnt stub of wax from the ledge where he had placed it on leaving the Silver Jackass earlier in the day and worked to get the wick lit. When he did, he took a hesitant step into the mine. He froze as a deadly sound reached his ears.

"The fuse is lit! I hear it sizzling!" Slocum dropped the candle and threw his arms around Happy Harry. He bulled from the mine, driving his partner back three steps before the invisible giant's fist closed around them, squeezing hard.

4

Slocum lifted his head and saw glowing eyes staring at him. He froze for a moment, then realized this only made the coyote bolder. Slocum let out a roar of anger that came out more as a strangled choking, but the sound convinced the predator to find dinner elsewhere. With a snarl, the coyote backed away and vanished into the night.

Night?

Slocum shook his head and thought something had come loose inside. Pain raced down his neck and throughout his back. He sagged forward, face in the dirt again. Lying there until he got his wits about him, Slocum rose and finally pieced together all that had happened.

His back burned like it had been set on fire. Reaching around, Slocum pulled away bits of burned canvas from his shirt. The charred odor was his own flesh, and the pain he felt was honestly earned. Groaning, Slocum began peeling off the offending garment, almost fainting from the pain as the strips peeled off bloody skin. Only when he was stripped to the waist and the cool night breeze blew around him, did Slocum fully revive.

''Harry? Where are you?'' Slocum struggled to his feet

and threw away his tattered shirt. In the dark he had trouble finding his partner. Happy Harry Harlan lay unconscious a few yards farther down the hillside. He had been knocked back by Slocum's mad rush, but the explosion had carried him away with even more force than it had Slocum.

From the way the miner lay, Slocum knew at least one leg was badly broken. Kneeling beside the grizzled man, Slocum cradled Happy Harry's head. Eyelids fluttered and watery eyes stared at him.

"Knew you were too tough to kill," Happy Harry said. "Thought I was too tough, but now I don't know. Feel real bad, John. Real bad."

"I took most of the blast," Slocum said, his back stinging as if a million paper wasps had attacked him. "You just busted up your leg trying to get away from the explosion." This caused Happy Harry to chuckle.

"Never could get the knack of turnin' tail and runnin'," he said. His face turned white as a wave of pain washed through him. "You figure they're gonna have to lop it off? My leg?"

"You and that miner from the Croaking Frog—McDermont—will be able to hang onto each other as you hobble around Virginia City from saloon to saloon," Slocum said, not seeing any damage serious enough to amputate the leg.

"What about Penks? He called out and then all hell cut loose on us."

Slocum had forgotten about their partner. For the first time, his green eyes moved up the littered slope to the mouth of the Silver Jackass. He heaved a deep sigh of resignation.

"If Penks is inside, it'll take be a cold day in July before we find him. The roof collapsed, from the first timbers on in, unless I miss my guess."

"Your guess is better than most people's expert opinion," Happy Harry Harlan said, falling back after trying to see what Slocum described. "That means we got to get to work and drill in, as if we were opening the shaft for the first time.''

"We know what's there," Slocum allowed. "That ought to give us spur.''

"We'll be rich 'fore the month's out, unless there's not much left. I don't seem to remember.''

Slocum shook his head again and felt new pain. He knew what Harry meant. It was hard to think through the red haze of pain from their injuries. He waited until his body settled back down to a level bearable enough for him to stand, then turned and trudged up the hill to the mouth of the mine.

The timbers had buckled or snapped under the blast. Penks had placed too large a charge inside the mine again. Or the charge had not been butted successfully up against the plug of rock they had wanted reduced to pebbles. Somehow, the blast had blown back out the mouth, taking with it the mine's pinnings.

Pushing at a few of the larger chunks of rock that had fallen, Slocum knew it would take serious drilling and blasting to get a new shaft sunk into the mountainside. If they ever found Penks's body, it would be a miracle. And right now, Slocum wasn't too inclined to spend much time looking for their worthless partner.

"The mine is good enough a grave for you, you worthless cayuse," Slocum said. He spat, getting grit and blood from his mouth. Arly Penks had robbed him of immediate wealth and that rankled, but worst of all, Penks had been incompetent. Slocum could tolerate a mite of laziness. When it came to stupidity and outright negligence, he figured Penks had finally claimed his due.

Walking slowly back and forth, he studied the side of the hill for any sign of cracking. Slocum frowned when he saw how the blast had opened a fissure to the left side of the original opening. Slocum ran his hand along the side of the crevice, then smiled. Getting back into the mine would be easier if they followed this crack in the rock. Parts of the tunnel might even be intact, letting them bypass weeks of backbreaking work.

"Slocum, you done upped and left me?"

"I wouldn't do that, Harry," Slocum shouted back. "I think we got our work cut out for us, but it's not as bad as it might have been."

"You mean that sorry son of a bitch couldn't even kill himself right?" Happy Harry laughed at this.

Slocum slipped and slid down the hill until he reached Happy Harry's side. Bending down, he got his arm around the miner's shoulders and heaved him erect. Slocum wobbled for a moment, then got Harry moving down the hill toward their shack.

"Don't need to rest, need my leg patched up," Happy Harry said. "Put me straightaway into the wagon and let's get to town. You look as if you have a powerful need for ol' Doc Hanley, yourself."

"Reckon I do," Slocum said. Slocum settled Happy Harry into the back of the wagon and made him as comfortable as possible before hitching up their donkey and getting the rig moving toward Virginia City. It took longer than he remembered getting to town, but they still arrived before midnight. Slocum reined back in front of the doctor's office and jumped to the ground. His knees gave way, and he had to catch himself. Then he regained strength and hurried inside.

Doc Hanley glanced up from his desk, where he sat reading a medical journal under a dim coal oil lamp.

"Can I help you?"

"Got an injured man outside."

"Got one in my office, too, from the look of your back," Hanley said, standing and coming around to peer at Slocum's back.

"Him first."

An hour later, Happy Harry's leg had been set and the man slept quietly on a cot at the side of Hanley's office.

Shards of rock had been pulled from Slocum's back and a dressing applied.

"You can wear this shirt. One of my patients left it as payment, and it doesn't fit me too well," the slender doctor said, holding up a huge red-checked flannel shirt.

"Thanks," Slocum said, gingerly inserting his arms into the sleeves.

"It'll be on the bill," Hanley said, smiling. "You *can* pay, can't you? After turning up your noses at two hundred ounces of silver, you *can* pay?"

"We can," Slocum said, remembering the lode of silver they had discovered. "Might take a spell, but we're good for the bill."

"I'm not too worried. Men who save others as you did at the Croaking Frog last night are seldom the ones who run out on their rightful debts and responsibilities."

"I'm feeling an attack of real responsibility right now. I need something that will make my back stop hurting."

"Take your pick," Hanley said, motioning across the street in the direction of four saloons. "There are plenty more within a hundred yards. A few shots of liquid fire will make you either numb or unconscious. In your condition, either would be a boon."

"Thanks, Doc. Reckon that's about the wisest prescription I ever got," Slocum said, slipping from the office. Happy Harry muttered in his sleep, then tried to roll over. The way his leg had been splinted prevented much movement. He wasn't going anywhere for a few days, or so Hanley had declared. That suited Slocum just fine. He had a powerful lot of thinking to do.

He stepped out into the cold night wind blowing off the mountains. Mount Davidson loomed like a dark giant, hiding its wealth under layers of rock. Slocum smiled crookedly as he thought how they had winnowed some of the silver from the tons of chaff. Rich. He and Happy Harry were rich. All they had to do was dig it out again.

Slocum sighed. Again he would spend long hours in the

cramped mine shaft scrabbling bits of precious ore from the earth. Or he could sell his share of the mine. The assay would show how rich the Silver Jackass really was and bring in offers from all comers. The thought of either Consolidated Virginia or Consolidated California bringing in bids turned him morose. He had no truck with the big companies.

They did things he would never cotton to if he lived to be a hundred. Their hydraulic mining ripped away entire mountains, washing the dirt into sluices and shaker tables. California had banned such mining techniques but not Nevada Territory. Not yet.

And their business practices were no better than their mining techniques. Slocum would have to watch himself carefully to keep from getting skinned, should he decide to sell to one of the big stock companies or their agents.

"Better to put in an honest day's work and keep the silver for myself," he said. He paused at the door of the saloon directly across the street from the doctor's office. The fight going on inside caused him to back off. He wasn't in any mood for the boisterous, good-natured brawls that sprang up in any mining camp. Life was hard, and blowing off steam with a round of fisticuffs kept many men happy.

Slocum wanted nothing but peace and quiet—and a full bottle of rye whiskey in front of him.

Walking down the middle of the street, he surveyed his choices both left and right. Most ran full tilt and he avoided them. But as he walked, he became increasingly uneasy. Once, he spun around and stared into the street behind him. A miner sailed through the open door of a saloon and landed heavily in the street, the saloon's bouncer making short work of his drunken patron.

But that wasn't what bothered Slocum. Ever since his days in the army during the war, he had listened to the feelings that warned of danger. That sense now shouted a warning, but he could not find the cause. Slowly turning in a circle, he studied the ramshackle saloons and cribs lining the street. Virginia City was an active, vibrant metropolis that had more than its share of lawbreakers.

The nightlife being played out around him was nothing he had not seen a thousand times before in a hundred other towns. Slocum shrugged it off as nothing more than delayed fear from the explosion. He had come within a hair of walking all the way into the mine and being blown up with Arly Penks.

"Maybe I ought to report his death to the sheriff," Slocum said aloud. He shook his head. There would be time later, when Happy Harry was up and able to confirm everything he told the law. Slocum had a few wanted posters dogging his trail and didn't want to run into a lawman who actually pawed through the stacks of warrants.

Slocum had been gut-shot during the war and had spent long months recuperating. By the time he returned to Slocum's Stand in Calhoun, Georgia, his parents were dead and a carpetbagger judge had taken a shine to the farm. No taxes had been paid, the Yankee judge had said. Pay up or get off, Slocum was told.

The judge and a hired gun had ridden in to take possession of the farm that had been in Slocum's family since the days of George I, before the revolution. And the judge had gotten the land in a way he had not expected.

John Slocum had ridden away that day so many years ago, two fresh graves on the ridge by the spring house. The law took a dim view of judge-killers, even when the killing was justified, and Slocum had spent his days one step ahead of that eternal warrant.

"Better to have Happy Harry with me when I report Penks's death," Slocum decided as he went into a quiet saloon. Two men lay passed out on a table at the rear, one man leaned against the bar talking with the saloon keeper, and four more played a diffident game of stud poker. They didn't even look up when he came in.

"What'll it be, mister?" called the barkeep, not budging from his spot at the other end.

"Whatever pours and doesn't cost too much." Slocum fished out a few crumpled greenbacks from his pants pocket.

"Got just what the doctor ordered," the barkeep said, pulling out a bottle of trade whiskey. Slocum shuddered. Whiskey with that tinge to it probably got its kick from gunpowder mixed with rusty nails, but he didn't care.

"It *is* what the doctor ordered," Slocum allowed, taking a big drink of the fierce liquor. He pushed across the folded greenbacks and didn't get any change, but he hadn't expected any. Most saloons discounted paper money and some refused to take any but their own coinage or silver.

Slocum leaned against the bar and drank steadily and silently. A few more men came in but they, too, were subdued compared to others in Virginia City. The only real disturbance came when the barkeep went to stoke the fire in the potbellied stove at the side of the saloon. The door caught and he burned his finger trying to pry it open to feed in more wood.

Slocum shivered a little in the cold. Even in the summer months, a chill settled in the high country. The mountains were treacherous: hot in the day and freezing cold at night. The small warmth put out by the stove was appreciated by all in the room.

The jingle of spurs drew Slocum's attention. No miner wore spurs and only a few of the bronc busters sported them when not astride a horse. These were favored more by wranglers—and gunmen.

The man standing in the door was dressed entirely in black. He pushed his cutaway coat back to reveal two pistols thrust into his belt. But the buckle, not the guns, caught Slocum's eye. The intricately fashioned buckle was of pure silver, shining like a small sun in the dimly lit saloon.

As if this flashy ornament wasn't enough, the gunman wore silver buttons on his coat and had spurs that sparkled as he walked slowly into the room. Silver conchos circled his hatband, and a few ran down the sides of his pants as if he was some vaquero come north. From the sallow complexion and pale eyes, though, Slocum knew this was no Mexican gunslinger.

The already quiet room turned into a tomb. Slocum shrugged it off and went back to drinking. Men like this enjoyed making a grand entrance. Give them the attention they craved and they would behave themselves—but that didn't mean Slocum had to get all het up over it.

Slocum figured the others were enough in awe of a man living by his quick reflexes to take any burden from his aching shoulders.

"Gimme a drink," the gunman demanded of the barkeep.

"Right away, sir. What's your poison? We got—"

"I'll take that bottle." He pointed a black leather gloved finger at the bottle in front of Slocum.

"That's his bottle. I got another here that—"

"That one," the gunfighter demanded in a cold voice.

"You mind, mister?" The barkeep's shaking hand reached out for the bottle. Slocum caught the man's wrist and pinned it to the bar. He didn't look at the barkeep. Instead, he turned toward the gunman. Slocum usually wore a Colt Navy in a cross-draw holster, but his pistol was back in the shack at the mine. He had not thought he'd have any call to use the ebony-handled weapon.

And he saw no reason now.

"I paid for it. You're welcome to a drink as my guest," Slocum said.

"Give me the entire bottle." The gunman stepped closer, pushing aside his coattails to free the butts of his two pistols. All Slocum could see was the dazzling silver buckle.

"Any reason you're being so disagreeable?" Slocum asked. "Folks around here are generous to a fault. And polite."

"You're calling me unmannerly?" The man stepped away from the bar and his hands clenched and unclenched as he readied to draw.

"I'm not wearing a gun," Slocum said, "but I doubt that matters much to a jackass like you."

The gunfighter's hands flashed for his pistols, but Slocum wasn't backing away. He stepped forward, his rock-hard fist driving squarely into the man's jaw. The black-clad man's head snapped back, and he fell to the floor, unconscious.

"Mister, that was the stupidest thing I ever saw," the barkeeper said breathlessly. "He was drawing down on you."

"With these?" Both pistols clattered onto the bar. Slocum had knocked out the man and then grabbed his weapons as he fell. "I don't think he knows how to use them."

He looked over his shoulder and saw the potbellied stove. Crossing the room in four long strides, Slocum popped open the door and heaved the six-shooters into the fire.

"Mister, those are loaded!" cried the barkeep as the first bullet went off from the heat. The bullets ricocheted around inside the stove until all twelve had fired. Slocum took one last drink from his bottle, then stepped over the slowly recovering gunslinger on his way out.

At the door Slocum turned and said to the groggy shootist, "If you want your guns, they're over there." And then he walked into the night, knowing he had made an enemy and not caring one whit.

5

Slocum stepped from the saloon and looked toward C Street. He heard the boisterous cries of drunken miners and the occasional staccato bark of six-shooters as enthusiastic revelers blew off steam from a hard day of working in the mines. He looked over his shoulder, saw nothing of the gunman intent on picking a fight, and then shook it off. He had been through too much today to take any guff off a man looking to make a reputation.

Still, Slocum worried a mite about the encounter. It wasn't likely a professional gunman would draw his guns on an unarmed miner to enhance his reputation. Some shootists were simply mean cayuses, but most had a code they followed, and it didn't include picking fights for no good reason. Shooting unarmed men got a fellow hanged, not applauded.

He dragged in a deep breath of the bitingly cold night air and shivered. When he left the Silver Jackass there had been no thought of a coat to protect himself against the freezing wind whipping down from the tall, snow-hidden peaks all around. When the Washoe zephyrs blew, the entire town turned downright arctic. Now he wished he had paused, just a moment or two, and brought along a blanket.

He took another deep breath of nighttime air, then held it. His eyes widened and Slocum looked around. He made a slow circle, then spun faster, sniffing the air like a hound dog on the trail of a fox. For a moment, Slocum couldn't figure what was wrong. Then memory hit him with the force of the roof of his mine collapsing on his head.

Fire!

Like a compass needle finds north, Slocum homed in on the source of the smoke.

"Doc Hanley's office is on fire!" he shouted at the top of his lungs. Slocum broke into a run, dashing in and out of the buildings to reach the front door of the office. Inside he saw the orange tongues of flame licking upward, following the walls as if they were a roadway for fire and going to the ceiling. It caused him to pause a few seconds at the sight. If Doc Hanley had decorated, he could not have hung a better curtain around his office.

Slocum kicked at the door to knock it open, but it resisted. He bounced back from the solid oak panel and tried again. This time the door tore free of the jamb and slammed inward, and Slocum almost died when the sudden rush of superheated air blasted at him as if he had opened a furnace door.

Throwing up his arm to protect his face, he ducked down and started into the fiery office, only to be driven back by another fierce blast. He drew the fire outward by keeping the door open and letting in air. From behind Slocum heard someone shouting at him. He tried to ignore it.

"Harry!" he shouted. "Can you hear me?"

Strong hands grabbed him. Slocum shoved away from them only to find more people clutching at his shirt. The floppy, red-checked shirt afforded them enough of a grip to drag him back from the raging inferno that the doctor's office had become.

"You can't go in there, mister. You're sure to singe your eyebrows if you even try." Slocum tried to fight, but he was knocked to the ground. He moaned in pain as he fell heavily on his injured back. But the pain focused him on the face of the man giving the orders.

Past the red shirt, Slocum's eyes went to the familiar face of the fire captain he had worked with the night before. The mutual recognition settled the dust between them.

"You're playin' hero again, aren't you, Slocum? Don't. Let us do our jobs. We're trained to put out fires like this and don't need much help this time around. We don't have to drag an engine all the way up to the divide. We've got our second-class Clapp and Jones coming."

Slocum heard the distant fire bell clanging loudly. And he became aware of others in the street outside Doc Hanley's office. The flames crept out the door and past windows, working avidly on the exterior walls. He tried to see what happened inside the office and couldn't. There was too much smoke.

"My partner's in there. Doc fixed him up, and he was sleeping on a cot." Slocum tried to stand, but two men grabbed his arms and pulled him away. He started to fight and then saw the look of determination on the fire captain's face. It brooked no argument.

"We need to know things like that, Slocum. Do you reckon the doc's in there with his patient?"

"I lost one partner already today. I'm not ready to lose another."

"Then put on a red shirt so we can find you in the confusion and get to work on the pump. Let the hose men get close to the fire. They know what to look for." The fire captain catapulted forward into Slocum's arms, knocking both men to the ground.

"The whole danged building's gone, cap'n," complained one fireman. "First water didn't mean nuthin' this time. If'n there's another explosion, we might lose every building along the street."

"What made the doctor's office blow like that?" Slocum went cold inside. He brushed himself off and got to his feet. The volunteer fireman stared at the inferno and shook his head.

"There's no telling what Hanley might have stored there. We've seen paint and beer go up like that. He was always trying out new drugs for folks. Some of them might have needed alcohol."

"If Happy Harry was in there, he's dead," Slocum said in a level voice. He tried not to lose hope, but experience had taught him that even friends and partners could die suddenly.

"Maybe Doc took him home with him. Hanley's been known to do things like that with his patients. All the time draggin' home the stray cats."

The well-intentioned lie hung in the hot air, then blew away. Slocum knew it would never happen that way. Harry Harlan had a broken leg. The doctor wasn't likely to move him around instead of just letting him rest until he regained his strength. From what Slocum could tell, Happy Harry wouldn't have been able to even stand on his broken leg for another few days.

"Get those pumps working," shouted the captain. "The fire's spreading. It—" He stumbled again as a new explosion blew apart the building next door to the doctor's office. This sent burning planks and fiery splinters sailing through the Virginia City night in a deadly rain. Slocum grabbed a red canvas fireman's shirt and slipped it on over the one Hanley had given him.

Then he went to work with determination. Putting out the fire single-handed was beyond him, but he could do the work of a dozen men. And he tried.

Lugging hoses was the least of the fight against the fire. The heavy Clapp and Jones steam pump had to suck from a tank and Virginia City was in a perpetual state of drought because of the demands of its residents for water. The river flowing along a few miles distant gave no help for fighting fires. Special reservoirs had been constructed and filled to supply the voracious appetites of the steam pump once it started, but Slocum found the first two empty. The hydrant system in this part of town was simply not working up to snuff.

"Try a reservoir tank over on F Street," someone suggested. "Drag along the hose. If you find it has any water in it, drop the hose in and signal." The man telling Slocum what to do hurried off in the opposite direction, also dragging a hose.

It turned into a race to find a cistern with enough water in it to matter. Slocum dropped to one knee and threw off the heavy cover to the buried tank. He saw nothing in the darkness, and the intense light from the fire made his night vision even worse. Instead of relying on sight, Slocum spat and listened. Even over the clangor of bells and the roar of the fire growing larger, he heard the distant splash.

Slocum lowered the hose quickly and then waved. He had found water first. The fireman manning the steam engine acknowledged his signal, then began turning valves and pulling levers. The hose snapped into a solid canvas pillar as it filled with water. Slocum watched the lump of water flow toward the distant pump as if a snake had swallowed a pig.

Then the firemen yelled a warning as water spewed from their shiny brass nozzle. Slocum saw the crew stagger as the hose bucked in their grip. He ran to help them.

"Stay out of the way. We got to save what we kin, and you'll jist be in the way," one fireman ordered. Slocum stared at Doc Hanley's office. Only charred wood remained. The second story had vanished, falling down onto the first floor in a mixture of charcoal, smoldering ashes, and more water than Slocum would have thought possible.

The volunteers already had turned their hoses in a different direction. They tried to save the assay office next door and failed quickly. The captain urged them to move on, to hose down other buildings threatened but not yet on fire. Slocum saw the wisdom in this, even as it doomed the county recorder's office with all its land deeds, a millinery, and a bookstore. When the paper records, the yards of cloth, and the books caught fire and blazed, it forced the firemen away.

"Ignore those fires," ordered the fire captain. "Keep your hoses on the surrounding buildings. If we don't stop the fire here, the whole danged D Zone's gonna go up!"

The steam pump began to fail. From the loud mechanical grating sounds filling his ears, Slocum thought he knew the problem. He had worked as an engine man on a Mississippi riverboat for a few months and had learned enough of walking beam engines to be of help.

"Let me give you a hand," he said, jumping onto the wagon bed beside a youth hardly into his teens.

"I don't know how the consarned thing works," the boy cried. "We just got it working this morning. All my pa told me to do was keep it fed. I throw in coal and steam comes out on top."

"The piston," Slocum said. "The piston's not been oiled properly. It seized up and has worked free of the cylinder." Picking up an ax handle lying in the wagon bed, Slocum thrust it between boiler and piston rod. Leaning back, he exerted all the force on the lever he could, but it refused to budge.

"I'll help you, mister." The youth grabbed the ax handle just below Slocum's hands. And Slocum felt the balky piston slowly moving back into the proper channel. With a final jerk, the piston rod snapped into place, and the engine began pumping properly again.

"That saved the whole danged block," the boy said. "My pa's gonna hear how you done saved us. Yes, sir, he will."

"Who's your pa?"

"Why, he's the captain of the Monumental Engine Company," the boy said proudly. Slocum nodded as he saw the family resemblance. "Captain Nate Chambers, the best danged fireman in the whole territory."

"A good man, your father," Slocum said. He gave the

boy a hand tossing lumps of coal into the firebox. When the pressure showed they were reaching the bursting point, Slocum held the boy back and let the machine continue its wild pumping. Rather than simply watch the steam engine pump, though, Slocum caught up the oil can and began squirting everywhere he saw moving metal. The screeching died down, and the major sounds came from the chuffing engine and the intense roar of the conflagration a block away.

Slocum fought the fire at the rear, but the jobs he performed were still vital to the effort of saving both D Zone and the rest of Virginia City. Slocum occasionally stared over the nightmarish scene and not once did he see any man slacking. The volunteers of Monumental Engine Company No. 6 battled a hungry enemy that could only be killed, never merely subdued.

"They got this one licked," the youth said with some pride. "It was more stubborn than a lot of 'em, but they got 'er, they did!"

Slocum nodded wearily when he saw the firemen tightening their nozzles and wading forward with axes to chop at the parts of buildings still standing. The blaze in the land office had proven worst of all, fed by the ton of paper inside. Slocum saw that most of the fancy wood filing cabinets had burned along with their contents.

He reached around and touched the scrap of paper folded and thrust into his rear pocket. The deed to the Silver Jackass was still safe and secure. And he knew Happy Harry and Arly Penks had copies, too.

The thought sobered him when he thought of his partners. They were gone. Both of them, leaving him sole owner of the richest mine he had ever seen in all his born days.

"Let some of the pressure out of the boiler," Slocum advised the boy. "No need to keep pumping at full steam."

"Yes, sir. I'll do that very thing." The boy smiled broadly when he let the steam out through the whistle release on top. Slocum wondered if the youth imagined himself the conductor on a train highballing through the countryside and whistling its way into each and every town.

It hardly mattered what went on in the boy's head. All Slocum felt was a hollowness inside that refused to go away. He walked through the ankle-deep mud and got to the doctor's office—or what remained of it.

Hesitating only a moment, he stepped into the office amid the burned timbers and the bits of soggy flooring that remained. The doctor's records had fed the fire, he saw. It almost seemed as if the records had been strewn all around for the fire's ravenous appetite.

He tossed aside fallen timbers from the upper floor, then tried to figure out where the cot that Happy Harry had slept in might have been. Slocum found himself turned around in the choking, barren black jumble of what had once been a prosperous doctor's office.

"Harry," he said in a low voice when he found his partner. The cot had turned to ash, but the skeletal remains told the tale. The miner with his broken leg had not been able to hobble to safety. Now his white bones were smudged with ash and lay like some steer out bleaching in the desert heat. Worst of all was the melted gold tooth in the skull that mocked Slocum.

"Smoke," came Doc Hanley's choked voice. "It's usually the smoke that makes 'em pass out. Nobody can move with lungs filled with smoke."

"Then he didn't feel it when he burned to death?"

"I didn't say that, son. I'm sorry. I saw how the two of you were good friends. Not like that with some partners." Doctor Hanley rested his hand on Slocum's shoulder.

"The whole town could have burned down," Slocum said, his mind turning in little circles and refusing to focus as it usually did. "Do you think he caused it?"

"Smoking?" Hanley shook his head. "It's possible. Did you see the fire come from here first?"

"I smelled smoke. By the time I got over here, the entire

building was in flames," Slocum answered. "The captain thought you might have taken him home with you."

"No, not this time. Because of his leg, I didn't think it would be prudent."

Slocum wanted someone to blame, but there was no one. Mining towns were notorious deathtraps. Fire was only one of the myriad dangers awaiting someone coming to the ore fields of the Comstock. How the fire started wasn't really too important.

"Who do I see about his burial? I'm not letting him be put down in the potter's field."

"I'll talk to Digger Conroy about it. Don't go worrying yourself none. Get some rest. That's the best thing you can do for yourself and everyone else."

Slocum nodded numbly. Everything crashed down on him as he walked slowly along the devastated street. Happy Harry dead: the doctor's office, the assay office, the land recorder's, the women's hat store, and four other businesses: all gone—all gone.

Slocum weaved slightly, as much from the new pain in his back as from fatigue and shock. He had gone too far, too fast, been through too much. And the few shots of rotgut back at the saloon were all he had eaten or drunk since before noontime. Slocum took hold of a pillar and rested his forehead against it, waiting for the dizziness hitting him to fade.

If anything, it got worse. He sank down onto the boardwalk, realizing he still had on the volunteer's red shirt. His hand touched his sooty hair.

"No helmet. I forgot to put on a fire helmet this time." Somehow this struck him as funny. He started to laugh until pain doubled him over again. Darkness crept in at the edges of his vision, but Slocum fought to keep from passing out. He had been through much the past few hours and would not yield. He would not give in.

"No, I won't," he said aloud.

"I think you should, sir. You are in no condition to simply lie about. Please, go to your home.''

"Don't have one," Slocum said, wondering who he was speaking to. He wiped dirt and soot from his eyes and found himself staring at a vision of loveliness. Never had Slocum seen a woman so lovely.

And then he passed out.

6

"Sir, allow me to help you. You appear to be half past dead." A strong arm circled Slocum's shoulders and pulled him to a sitting position. Slocum heard a gasp as the young woman drew away. He almost toppled over. He caught himself and remained in a sitting position, the world spinning around him.

"Your back! You are bleeding. And you are covered with soot and ash."

"I fought the fire. My partner died in it," Slocum managed to say. He closed his eyes, fought the world whirling around him, then added, "And I haven't had much to eat today."

"You poor thing. Please, sir, I insist. Allow me. Will you be all right if we go to a restaurant and get something to eat?"

Slocum squinted and saw the pale fingers of dawn creeping along the ridge of the mountains to the east. He had been up all night and had not realized it. So much had happened. So damned much. And none of it was particularly good.

Except this lovely woman, her long, dark hair flowing in

51

gentle waves down her back and her bright sapphire eyes staring so boldly at him. He heard the culture in her voice and saw it in her posture. And her elegant clothing seemed entirely out of place in a rough-and-tumble mining camp like Virginia City.

"You're from back East," Slocum said. "Boston? No, maybe New York."

"You have a good ear for accents, sir." She averted her eyes slightly, as a proper young lady would. "I hail from Philadelphia."

"Your kindness is appreciated, but there is no reason for you to pay for my meal. I can—" Slocum patted his pockets, hunting for money. He had a few greenbacks folded in his shirt pocket, but the water from the hoses had completely soaked him, in spite of the fireman's red canvas shirt he still wore over the checkered shirt.

"Don't trouble yourself. I know what it is like to be down on your luck. I have been there myself some years ago. And truthfully, there is a compelling reason I make the offer of breakfast to you. I need your assistance in a personal matter."

"Whatever I can do." Slocum took a few hesitant steps and grew stronger as he walked. The woman was taller than he had thought at first, the top of her hat even with his eyes.

"I found a decent restaurant at the end of the street. Such a disaster this night! I hope the place is not damaged by the fire."

"Only along the street farther south was there any damage," Slocum said.

"You fought the fire?"

"I helped. I'm not a volunteer. I discovered the fire and tried to do what I could to put it out. My partner died in that fire."

Slocum's thoughts wandered back to how Happy Harry had died. If he had been quicker, if he had not taken the doctor's advice to go get a drink, if—

Slocum shook his head. If regrets were gold double eagles, he would have been rich years ago. He couldn't blame himself for not being with Happy Harry and helping him from the burning building. He had done as much as he could and no man could do more, whether for a partner or a relative.

That thought sent him back years and years, to the war. He had been a sniper and his brother had ridden alongside that damned fool Pickett. There might have been a moment at Gettysburg when Slocum could have saved his brother Robert, but he doubted it. All the years of playing the battle over and over had never saved his brother. His hand touched the pocket watch riding in his pants watch pocket. That was the sole legacy from Robert.

"You are lost in thought, sir. Perhaps there is something more I can do to help you?"

"You are too kind," Slocum said. He was rewarded with a shy smile that fluttered at the corners of the young woman's lips. He held the door for her as they went into the small café. The owner looked up and saw Slocum's condition, then sniffed hard at the heavy odor of woodsmoke surrounding him. For a moment, Slocum thought the man was going to order him out. To his surprise, the man rushed forward and smiled broadly.

"One of the firemen from the Monumental Engine Company? Please, come this way. Let me fetch you some coffee. You did a fine night's work, savin' half the town from going up in a blaze. What else can I get for you?"

Slocum was taken aback. He was more used to being thrown out of respectable places instead of invited in and received as a hero.

"Coffee for both of us," Slocum ordered. "And I'll need a few minutes to look at a menu."

"Certainly, sir, certainly. And keep up the good work. We all appreciate it." The man slapped Slocum on the back. Slocum winced but said nothing about the pain. The restaurant owner was only being civil.

"You are well thought of in town," the woman said, her blue eyes appraising him anew.

"A change for me," Slocum muttered. He sipped at the hot, black coffee and let it restore some measure of his strength.

"I am too forward. I should not ask you for help. I do not even know you."

"John Slocum's the name. I own a mine a few miles down the road," Slocum said, his mind turning over the fact that he was now sole owner of the Silver Jackass. He had never heard either of his partners talk about relatives who might inherit their shares, but then none of them had thought they would die after they got rich.

"Excellent," she said, beaming. The woman pushed a vagrant strand of her dangling midnight-black hair from her bright blue eyes. "I need to find someone who is also a miner. A relative of mine. If you are similarly employed, you must know him."

"The hills are filled with men doing nothing but digging," Slocum said. "I have only been in town a few weeks, myself. Have you asked around Virginia City already?" Slocum finished the coffee and got another steaming cup. He ordered food and so did the woman, Slocum feeling only slightly guilty about her paying for his meal. He had the money. It would simply require a few minutes with a hot iron to dry out the soaked greenbacks in his pocket.

"I have. There is no central agency where I could inquire, however. I asked the sheriff—Sheriff Tyler is his name—and he said he knew nothing of my brother. My half brother, actually. He is a miner and came West many years ago."

"Can't be too many years. You're not that old," Slocum said. The woman appeared to be no more than twenty.

"My brother—half brother—is almost twice my age. His mother died in childbirth, and our father remarried."

"Your mother?"

"Yes, sir. Exactly right. But Arlin left Philadelphia when I was only eight. I hardly remember him."

"Why are you looking for him now? Life in Philadelphia has to be a sight easier than here in Virginia City." Slocum began cutting the steak set in front of him, alternating between the meat and the fried potatoes on the side. He reserved the fried eggs for later, when his appetite was sated and he could appreciate the full flavor.

"Our father recently passed on," the dark-haired woman said. She sniffed slightly, taking a lace handkerchief from her clutch purse and dabbing at her eyes. If another had done this, it would have appeared contrived. With her, it seemed both natural and expected that her feelings would run deep.

"So you're hunting for your only blood relative? For what reason?"

"Father asked that I bring Arlin his forgiveness. On his deathbed he asked me to reconcile with my brother and tell Arlin no hard feelings existed when Father passed away."

"If there is any inheritance, I'd suggest you keep it safe and sound in Philadelphia and not worry about someone who left twelve years back."

"There is little enough. I have a small annuity that meets many of my needs. All I need do is find Arly and give him my father's message. But he is so hard to find!"

"Arly?" Slocum froze, fork with a piece of steak halfway to his mouth. "Thought you said your half brother's name was Arlin."

"Arly is a nickname. Oh, forgive me, please. In the rush, I have forgotten my manners. You introduced yourself, but I failed to do so. My name is Cara Penks."

"Arly Penks is your half brother?" Slocum said, startled. He thought he had all emotion burned out of him in the past day. He was wrong.

"You know him!"

Slocum put the fork down and looked around the café

which was slowly filling with morning customers. This hardly seemed the place to tell Cara that her only surviving relative had just died, but he didn't know what would be a better venue.

"I've come to surprise Arly. He's so much older than I, but still, I know he will be happy to see his only sister." Cara's voice trailed off when she saw the grim expression on Slocum's face. "What's wrong, Mr. Slocum?"

"Arly Penks is—was my partner," he said. He took a quick gulp of the hot coffee. It seared his throat, but he hardly noticed. The joy on Cara's lovely face tore at his heart more than the coffee burned his mouth.

"Wonderful! Where can—" Cara's face turned into a mask of horror when she realized what Slocum had said earlier involved her half brother. "He's dead. He's the one who died in the fire!"

"No, not then. It was an accident at the mine. He died in an explosion when we were blasting a plug of rock. Harry Harlan and I were hurt. I brought Happy Harry in, and he died in the fire last night."

"Oh, no!" she said, looking stricken. Slocum expected the tears to flow, but they did not. Cara Penks was past tears. Shock held her in its tight grip.

"I'm sorry. I wish there was some way to break the news to you more gently." He reached over and touched her hand. Cara stared at him, as if she had left the world and was lost in her own thoughts.

"I'm sorry. This wasn't what I expected, yet in a way, I think I did. Father heard nothing from Arly over the years, nothing except for one letter. And an old friend of the family saw Arly here in Virginia City a few months ago and wrote to tell us. That's how I happened to come here. But Father always thought it possible Arly was dead, and I must have considered that, also."

"You almost got out here in time. It was only yesterday afternoon when he died."

"His body?" Cara Penks sniffed a little now, but still

no tears came. Slocum saw the steel center in the woman and knew she was no hothouse flower. She had been rocked by death in the past and accepted her half brother's now.

"In the mine. There might never be a way of getting to it. He set a charge that went off when we all least expected it. It killed him, broke Harry's leg, and cut up my back."

"Your back," she said. "I am much obliged to you, Mr. Slocum. But I have been so self-centered. You have conveyed all I wanted from you and just over a meal. I didn't realize my trip would end so quickly. But your back is once again bleeding. Even on the red shirt I see new spots of blood."

Slocum tried to move and winced. She was right. The wounds had broken open during the night of strenuous effort.

"I'll get the doc to tend to it again. He patched me up pretty good before."

"Nonsense. I owe you something for this information about Arlin. Please allow me to order a hot bath for you at the bathhouse next to my hotel, the International House. It is quite nice, with gaslights and an elevator, and it seems to be the tallest building in town. I shall tend to your injury in way of payment for your information."

"That's mighty kind of you but not necessary."

"Please, Mr. Slocum. I need to feel I am of some use to someone. And I did tend my father those last few months. I became quite an accomplished nurse."

"I'm sure you did." Slocum quickly finished the food on his plate. Even the promise of getting his back cleaned and bandaged would not drive him away from filling his belly. He stood and dug in his pocket for the wad of greenbacks. He dropped it on the table when he saw Cara making no move to pay. The revelation of her only remaining relative's death had shaken her.

But Slocum was startled again when the café owner scooped up the money and thrust it back into Slocum's shirt pocket. "Keep it. Just remember my fine establishment next time there's a fire."

"I will," Slocum said, nodding vaguely, more worried about Cara than the restaurant owner. He hurried after the young woman, catching up with her halfway across the street.

"There is the bathhouse," she said. "For a quarter you can get hot water and for another dime they will furnish soap."

"You don't have to do this, Miss Penks."

"Call me Cara. Please, John. Please. I am so at ends I do not know what to do or where to go."

She took his arm and steered him toward the bathhouse. The proprietor hardly batted an eye when Cara ordered the hot water in a private room and lots of clean bandages. The request was nothing out of the ordinary, and somehow, the sight of the red fireman's shirt made everything just fine with him.

"There," Cara said after seeing to pouring the hot water into a huge brass tub with a high back. "Cleanse yourself and I shall see to sterilizing the bandages."

Slocum waited for her to leave, then peeled off his filthy clothing. The shirt he had gotten from Doc Hanley stuck in places to his back, causing him to wince. He finally decided to soak off the shirt. Naked save for the shirt dried onto his back, he slid into the tub. The warmth seeped into his muscles and immediately worked to relax him. His eyes shot open when Cara came bustling back into the room carrying a pile of white rags.

"John, I—Oh! I didn't know. I mean, I hardly realized." Cara Penks stopped and lifted her eyes to stare at him. Something shifted within her. Slocum saw resolve harden. She came forward and knelt beside the tub. "I'll be gentle peeling off the shirt."

Slocum said nothing as her long fingers pried the shirt from his wounds. And he sighed softly when she began laving his back. But his eyes came wide open when her bathing moved to other parts of his body. Under the surface of the soapy water he felt himself hardening as her touch excited him.

"You need me," she whispered softly in his ear. "I can tell."

"Is this what you want?" Slocum asked. He could hardly believe what she suggested. She was a proper young lady from Philadelphia. Then he realized she had also lost her anchor in the world and floated aimlessly. She was reaching out for a new purpose in her life. And she held Slocum firmly in her hand to be sure she would get it.

"It's more than that, John. It's what I need." The way Cara spoke, the words told Slocum she was not fooling herself. This was no romantic notion that had fluttered into a sweet young thing's mind. It was part of a healing process for a full-bodied, hot-blooded woman.

Her mouth brushed across his, then she moved closer and kissed with a fervor that told of the intense emotions imprisoned within her. She needed release, and Slocum was going to give her that. And in doing so, he would share in the release of his own feelings.

Water sloshed over the rim of the tub, getting Cara's skirt wet. She pushed back and quickly stripped it off. Then she pulled off her petticoats and stood clad from the waist down only in her frilly undergarments. She smiled wickedly, then turned as if in modesty. But what she did was completely wanton. She bent slightly, her rump tightening. She slipped off her pantaloons, slowly revealing the curving white moons of her buttocks and giving just a hint of the paradise lurking between her milky white thighs.

Looking back around one side, she said, "See anything you like?"

Slocum surged from the tub and caught her around the waist. As he pulled her back, she slipped and fell into the tub, sitting on his lap. Slocum kissed and bit at her neck, then reached around and caught both her full breasts. He began crushing them as his passion mounted. He felt the hard buttons of her nipples through the layers of cloth still hiding them.

"More, John, give me more. I *need* more," Cara sobbed softly. She put her hands on the side of the tub and hoisted herself. Reaching down into the warm water, she found his manhood and positioned it underneath her body. Then she sank back, taking his full length.

Slocum gasped as hot female flesh surrounded him. Cara twisted slightly from side to side, which forced Slocum to concentrate on not performing like a young buck with his first woman. Cara's movement up and down, twisting slightly as she rose and fell in the water, almost robbed him of his control.

When she bent forward, her buttocks slipped into the curve of his loins and he sank even deeper into her. Cara began rocking, moving up and down his hard length, building friction with every slight swaying motion of her hips.

"I can't keep going much longer. You're too exciting," Slocum said. He had been through too much to appreciate fully the gift he received. And yet he was not going to shoo her away, hoping there might be a chance later with her. He knew culture and class when he saw it. After Cara Penks worked through her distress, she would return to Philadelphia and he would never see her again.

It was selfish, but Slocum wanted this moment to last forever, no matter how weak his flesh might be.

"I'm all alive inside, John. I feel sensations creeping up on me. So nice, so nice. Oh!" She gasped and began splashing water out of the tub with her increasingly frantic movements. She reached into the water and cupped his balls, teasing them with her fingertips. Then she squeezed hard, and Slocum was lost. The fiery tide of his passion exploded just as Cara threw back her head like a bucking bronco and cried out in her own desire.

They moved together for another few seconds, then Slocum sank back into the tub. He had been exhausted in his life, but never had it felt this good. His body had been drained of all energy by his exertions, carnal and otherwise.

The sight of Cara rising out of the tub was almost enough to get him hard again. Almost. She grabbed a towel and dried her privates, then rubbed down her long, slender legs.

"Allow me to finish what I started. Your back requires immediate attention."

"Yes, ma'am," Slocum said. "Whatever you say."

As if they had not just made love in the tub, Cara Penks began bandaging him. And then, as he dressed, she settled her skirts about her and left the room. Slocum wondered if he would ever see her again. By the time he was dressed in his rags and had stepped into the warm morning sun, Cara Penks was gone.

7

The sun heated Slocum's face. For a moment he stopped and let the warmth seep into his body. His back was bandaged and feeling good, his belly was filled, and he had just spent a delightful hour with a lovely, willing, and totally wanton young lady. Slocum scanned the street once more for any sign of Cara Penks, but she had vanished as surely as half the buildings farther down the street.

Seeing the aftermath of the fire, Slocum walked slowly in that direction. The night had veiled most of the destruction. The morning light brought out the stark horror of what had happened. Timbers still smoldered in places, and building after building had collapsed into itself. Not a single two-story structure remained in the area around Doc Hanley's office. Even if the buildings hadn't been touched directly by the flames, the water from the firemen's hoses had knocked huge holes in the flimsy walls.

"I lost everything," a woman moaned. She stood in the street near the millinery. She wrung her hands as a man beside her tried to console her. "Everything is gone."

"Easy, Martha," the man soothed. "We been burnt out before. We lost a wagon to a flash flood. We even lost poor little Emma. We kept a-goin' and we will again.''

"We can help get the walls up 'fore you know it," another man offered. "The whole block is going to be knocked down. We can save some of the timber. That way you don't have to freight in more from over in Tahoe.''

As they continued making their plans, Slocum wandered on. Tragedy was everywhere, and he realized how expensive the small fire had been. The slopes of Mount Davidson had long since been stripped bare of all timber for the mines. Most of the planking used in Virginia City came from miles away. Maybe the sawmills to the southwest in Carson City furnished some of the wood, but Slocum knew that would be expensive to transport.

He would have to find out soon if he wanted to sink a new shaft at the Silver Jackass.

Thinking of the mine sent his feet in the direction of Doc Hanley's office, but he could not make himself go through the ruins to the burned cot where Happy Harry had died. Instead, he turned to the recorder's office two doors away. If anything, the fire there had been even more intense when the file cabinets caught fire.

Two men pawed through the records—or what remained of them.

"Can I lend a hand?" called Slocum. He rubbed his nose at the heavy smoke odor hanging in the air. From what he could see, every cabinet had been spilled out and its contents destroyed.

"Thanks, mister, but we don't need it.''

"How'd the cabinets get emptied out like that?" asked Slocum frowning. Though the fire had been more intense here, he wondered how the filing cabinets had been opened and the records strewn about as if someone had sought something before the fire started. "You must have had one sloppy clerk.''

"I'm the clerk," the man snapped. "Don't know how this happened 'less it was the firemen coming in to dig around.''

Slocum knew he still wore the bright red fireman's shirt. He thought back. He had fought the steam pump and found water and then worked with the hose teams. It took him a spell, but he remembered how the men with axes had worked through the buildings—and no one had been able to get into the recorder's office. The fire had been too hot.

"Nobody could get inside," Slocum said. "From the heat, the fire fed straightaway on your files. You have copies of these?"

"Copies of all the land deeds are also stored up in Carson City," the clerk told him. "And the mine owners have their copies." He peered at Slocum. "You own property in these parts? You look familiar."

Slocum fished in his hip pocket for the deed to the Silver Jackass. He pulled out a ruined sheet of yellow foolscap. Wear had creased and flattened it, but water from fighting the fire had destroyed any hope of reading what had been written on the paper. Slocum held it up.

The clerk sneered. "No way that will stand up in a court of law," he said. "I can't even swear it came from my office."

"My partners have copies," Slocum said. *Had* copies, he mentally corrected. Where Happy Harry and Arly Penks would have kept their copies of the land deed was unknown, but he would find out soon enough. The shack where they had shared their lives for almost a month was too small to hide much, including memories.

"Get your ass on up to Carson City and have the state recorder give you a copy," advised the clerk. "It's going to be months 'fore I get back into business. Hell, look at that." He pointed to a small knot of prospectors standing down the street.

"You have business," Slocum said, recognizing the way the men shifted their feet nervously, anxious to get their new claims recorded properly so they could get to work pulling silver from the ground.

The clerk snorted. "Won't do 'em any good 'less they

have an assay. And there's not going to be anything but field assay done for a spell." The clerk pointed to the building next door to his ruined office.

Slocum shrugged and walked on, kicking at the debris littering the street. He didn't know who was responsible for cleaning up after a fire, but they had yet to start their work. Stopping in front of the assay office told him nothing had been saved there. Through the burned flooring he saw dirt and little else. The chemicals used by the chemist had fed the fire along one wall. Frowning, Slocum went and examined the remains but couldn't put his inchoate thoughts into words.

Shaking himself, he left the devastation and walked back down the street in the direction of the bathhouse. Cara Penks had said her hotel was nearby. There were only two hotels, and one Slocum immediately ignored. It had the look of a whorehouse to it, and not the sort of place a lady like Cara Penks would stay. The other was five stories tall. He remembered her comment about the International Hotel being the tallest in town.

In the lobby of the hotel, Slocum looked around. The carpet was impeccable, the place was clean, and the clerk behind the desk alert.

"Help you?" he called.

"I'm looking for Miss Cara Penks. There's something important she ought to know." Slocum was aware of how he looked, even after the bath. The clerk eyed him critically, then came to a conclusion.

"Set yourself down over there, and I'll send a bellboy to see if she's seeing anyone."

Slocum settled in a high-backed chair and watched as the clerk dragged a towheaded boy from a side room. The clerk spoke quickly to the boy and sent him racing up the stairs to the second floor. Slocum leaned back and closed his eyes, his body reminding him how long it had been since he had slept.

He drifted off, only to come awake when he heard the

soft swish of a woman's skirts.

"Mr. Slocum," Cara said. She seemed distant and cold compared to the way she had been before. He knew she was trying to accept her half brother's death so soon after losing her father. And maybe she felt a little guilty about what the two of them had done in the bathhouse.

"Miss Penks," he said, getting to his feet. "I didn't want us to part so abruptly."

"That is most kind of you, sir, but I felt the need to pack and prepare for my immediate return to Philadelphia. There is nothing to keep me in Virginia City now that you tell me my brother has passed on." She stood with her hands clutched tightly at her waist. Between her fingers she worried her lace handkerchief.

"Might be," Slocum said. He pulled out his ruined copy of the deed for the Silver Jackass and held it out. "This is the deed to our mine. I need to get a copy."

"Yes?" Cara's distant reply told him she was already halfway back East.

"I don't recall Happy Harry ever mentioning a relative. Fact is, Arly never mentioned any kinfolk, either, but you're here." Slocum fought fatigue to put his thoughts into the proper words. "Although a woman can't own real property, it seems only fitting that you inherit your brother's share of the mine."

"A third of the mine?"

Slocum paused for a heartbeat. "Might be half the mine, since there's just you and me left. Partners get clear title to property in the case of death."

"Then you are entitled to the entire mine, Mr. Slocum," she said. "I have no desire to root about in the ground to find a few specks of gold or silver."

"There's more than a few nuggets, Cara," he said in a low voice. "There's enough black dirt in that mine to make you rich. Make us both rich."

"You would share this with me?" Cara's attention came back and fixed on Slocum. "There's no need. You and

Arlin and your Happy Harry found this claim and worked it. You deserve the results of your labor. I have done nothing to deserve it.''

"I wouldn't say that," Slocum declared, smiling. "You came along and offered help when I needed it. And you are Arly's kin. If necessary, I can sell the mine and give you half. It would go for a princely sum.''

"Mr. Slocum, I don't know what to say. This is generosity far beyond anything I accorded you. Perhaps it is right what they say. 'Cast your bread upon the water for thou shalt find it after many days.' ''

"You don't have to wait that long," Slocum said. He became increasingly anxious to get back to the mine shack to find his partners' copies of the precious deed. "When can you travel out to the Silver Jackass to look it over?''

"Why, right away. I was preparing for travel.'' She stared at his rough clothing and frowned. "I am not up to desperate travel, I fear. Should I find something less refined?''

"I can find a carriage, if you like. I brought Happy Harry into town in a wagon, but that might be too uncomfortable for you.''

"Don't worry about that, Mr. Slocum. I can survive about anything after the past few hours.''

"I hope not everything was a trial for you," Slocum said. The twinkle in Cara's blue eyes and the small smile that sneaked onto her ruby lips told him she had enjoyed certain parts of their meeting.

"I'll be ready in a few minutes. Pick me up at the front steps?''

Slocum hurried off to the livery and found the wagon and the jackass that pulled it. The stable hand accepted a dime for his effort and went back to his chores as Slocum hitched up the balky animal. He got the jackass moving in the direction of the hotel, wondering if Cara would be waiting as she said. It was as if a new sun rose over Slocum and warmed him when he saw the dark-haired beauty patiently standing on the hotel's broad front porch.

"You seem surprised to see me, John," she said as he helped her onto the wagon box.

"It occurred to me as I was driving over that you might not want to see the place where your brother died." Slocum watched her reaction carefully.

"I can tolerate it. In a way, I *want* to see the mine. I know so little of such matters." She sat primly, hands folded in her lap. She jerked back slightly as Slocum snapped the reins onto the jackass's rump and got it moving slowly down the road. He longed for a strong horse to pull the wagon, but his partners—primarily Arly Penks—had not wanted to spend the money. The jackass had proven strong and reliable for the work required of it.

"There's not much to see any longer, not after the explosion. The entire mine shaft came tumbling down."

"That's all right. I understand your reasons. You want me there to corroborate that you found my brother's deed—and your other partner's—fair and square. Is that the proper phrase?"

"It surely is," Slocum said. They rode along in the bright sunlight, lost in their own concerns. Slocum couldn't keep from wondering about Cara Penks and what she thought of him. Their meeting had been peculiar, and it had only gotten stranger, not that Slocum would have changed one instant of it. But what did Cara think of him?

She did not seem to blame him for her half brother's death. Slocum kept his own counsel on that. He would have throttled Arly Penks for his sloppy work blasting in the mine if the careless miner hadn't blown himself up first. Fact was, he had never much liked Penks, but Happy Harry had insisted they needed the third man's expertise in using explosives.

"Is that the way to the mine?" Cara's soft voice shook Slocum from his reverie. They had driven for miles, and he hardly realized it. He blinked and pulled down the brim of his Stetson to see the crude sign pointing into the hills.

"That's our claim," Slocum agreed. The jackass was already straining at the harness to go up the road. Slocum let the animal have its head. The strong beast knew how best to pull them.

"This is exciting," Cara said. "I have never seen a mine before."

"You won't see much here, but . . ." Slocum's voice trailed off. He saw evidence that someone had ridden along the road since he had taken Happy Harry into Virginia City. Claim jumpers roved the hills, waiting for a mine to be deserted for even a short time. A team of them moved in and tried to bull their way into full possession. With the deed office in Virginia City in a smoking ruin, any claim jumper would find it that much easier to take over a silver mine by force of arms.

Slocum's hand drifted to his left side, but the cross-draw holster he usually wore wasn't there. While working in the mine, a side arm got in the way. Slocum had left the holster and his Colt Navy wrapped up in oilcloth with the rest of his gear.

"Is something wrong, John?" Cara craned her slender neck as she studied the countryside, trying to figure out what had spooked him so.

"Maybe nothing," Slocum said. "We might have a visitor at the mine."

"This is a remote location. Do you have people dropping by often?"

"Never," he said. Slocum was pleased to see that his real meaning wasn't lost on her. Cara bit her lower lip and nodded. As she did so, a bit of her black hair slipped free of her hat. She unconsciously brushed it away in a quick, nervous gesture he had come to associate with her.

"I don't expect trouble," Slocum said, "but it won't hurt to be ready for it."

"But you have no weapon."

"We'll pull off the road here, and I'll go ahead on foot. You stay with good old Vic."

"Vic? Oh, you mean your mule."

Slocum didn't bother correcting her. Vic didn't like being called a mule, but the animal's feelings wouldn't be hurt any by letting him stop his uphill hauling. He would have a chance to crop at the dry grass growing alongside the road.

Jumping to the ground, Slocum started walking in a distance-devouring stride. After less than ten yards, he paused, turned, and stared at Cara sitting on the wagon box, so lovely and proud and elegant in the hot Nevada sunlight. A quick tip of his hat in her direction and he was off, following the contour of the land until he came to an arroyo. Ducking beneath the high banks cut by spring runoff, Slocum made his way toward the Silver Jackass. He passed a spot where they had dug their small sweet water well. Slocum knelt and looked carefully at the sunbaked ground around the well, hunting for spoor.

"Nothing," he said. Slocum wasn't sure what that meant, other than that the visitor to the mine hadn't been thirsty.

Staying low and taking advantage of what cover he could find in the sparse vegetation, he came within a dozen yards of the mining shack. Listening hard, he tried to decide if anyone lay in wait. A claim jumper might want to bushwhack an unsuspecting miner returning to the mine, but hardly anyone knew the Silver Jackass held a huge fortune. Penks and Happy Harry had died before they had a chance to brag about it in town, and Slocum was always close-mouthed about his business.

Creeping forward on his belly, every sense alert for attack, Slocum slowly acknowledged the sensation of being completely alone in the camp. A sudden flash caused him to freeze. It took a second for him to find the source of reflected light high on the mountain, about where he had seen Penks a couple of days earlier.

Slocum shielded his eyes and tried to make out who wandered about up there but couldn't. He scrambled to his feet and covered the distance to the shack in only a few seconds. The cabin had no windows. Slocum went to the door and saw how it had been kicked down. It hung on one leather hinge, partially hiding the dark interior of the cabin.

Spinning around the edge of the broken door, he jumped into the shack, ready to fight his weight in wildcats.

Whoever had preceded him into the camp had left some time back, but not until after searching the cabin and leaving everything scattered about. Somehow, Slocum knew exactly what would be missing from his and his partners' belongings.

"The deeds," he muttered, after a quick search of his own. "Harry's and Penks's deeds are gone."

8

The grating of feet against gravel behind him caused Slocum to drop into a gunfighter's crouch and spin about. His hand went for the Colt Navy he usually carried at his left hip, but the hand groped on thin air. Then Slocum saw that Cara Penks had come up from where he had left her down on the road.

"You are very fast," Cara said, staring at him wide-eyed. She blinked when he stood and let his hand relax. There was no gun in his grip, and she didn't know what else to say.

"I don't know if claim jumpers came through or just sneak thieves," Slocum said. He pointed into the shack. Cara moved closer. Slocum sucked in his breath and held it. The young woman's perfume rose to his nostrils and set his heart pounding. The feel of her firm breast pushing against him and the sunlight shining off her dark hair turning her into an angel come to earth combined to send his thoughts cartwheeling in a dozen different directions. Her sharp voice brought him back to the reality of the mining camp.

"Thieves!" she cried. "They are everywhere. You

73

would not believe how evil they can be in Philadelphia. And here! I thought everyone on the frontier was honest.''

''Only as long as you've got 'em square in your gun sight,'' Slocum said. The mention of his six-shooter caused Slocum to explore the shack again. He had not left his weapon out in plain sight. In fact, he had not bragged to either of his partners that he even wore a six-gun most of the time. Since coming to work at the Silver Jackass Mine, there had been no call to carry it.

Dropping to one knee, Slocum heaved his bunk away from the wall and burrowed down into the hard dirt where he had placed an oilcloth-wrapped package. His fingers closed on the familiar outline of the Colt and its holster.

''Did you find something, John?''

''Not everything of value was taken,'' Slocum said. ''They left me some of my belongings.'' He didn't burden her with the knowledge of what he had found untouched. With the sparse gear remaining to him after the thief—or thieves—had finished with the shack, Slocum stepped back into the bright sun.

His gaze went higher on the slope to the point where Penks had prowled around before the explosion. There was no flash of silver now. Did the sun move away from something dropped there on the ground or had the person sporting the silver—like a badge?—moved on?

''Is something wrong? Other than the sneak thief?'' Cara sounded worried there might be further trouble. Slocum reassured her they were alone and in no danger.

''You can poke around all you like,'' he told her. ''Don't touch anything that looks like it might blow up. I don't know where Arly stored the spare black powder he used in the mine.'' As he spoke, Slocum frowned. He slowly realized how little he knew about his dead partner and how he conducted his business. The lure of the riches in the Silver Jackass had blinded him to too many questions he would have asked otherwise—and gotten answers for.

''Where are you going?''

"Up the hill to look around. I won't be long." He paused, then added, "There's no need for you to go to the mine. It collapsed and there's nothing to see there. Nothing." Slocum found himself more concerned for her than he should be. Cara Penks was a woman who had simply waltzed into his life and nothing more. He had no call to try to protect her from the scene of her brother's death.

"I will stay here. Or ought I return to the wagon?" Cara turned this way and that, suddenly confused.

"The going will be rough where I'm heading. Stay here where you can keep me in view." Slocum started up the hill, carrying the oilcloth package with his six-shooter. He didn't unwrap it until he was sure Cara couldn't see what he did. Slocum had no idea why he wanted to keep it from her that he was well-schooled in the use of a six-gun, but he did.

"She's been through hell already," he muttered to himself. "Don't frighten her any more."

Puffing from the exertion, Slocum scrambled up the hillside. He tried to find the path Penks had taken but could not. The terrain was too rough and uneven. Now and then Slocum glanced over his shoulder down at the shack where Cara waited. He saw how she paced to and fro like a caged animal. Her impatience conveyed itself to Slocum. He had no idea why he bothered to climb the steep hill, other than to satisfy himself that no one roamed around up there.

He judged distances and locations and began carefully searching for any spoor when he reached the level spot where he reckoned Penks had been, if it had even been Penks. Neither he nor Happy Harry had identified their partner on the hill. All Slocum found after careful study was a patch of prickly pear cactus, two anthills, and more lizards than he could shake a stick at. Slocum pushed his Stetson back and wiped his forehead. Sweat soaked into his shirt, plastering the cloth to his flesh, and turned his back as prickly as the cactus he carefully stepped over every time he ranged around the area.

"Can't keep going like this," Slocum decided. His mouth had turned to cotton, and he was in sore need of a drink of water from his well. And leaving Cara alone too long didn't seem like a good idea. She was a high-strung filly and might do something foolish.

Like speak to a stranger more dead than alive lying on a boardwalk in Virginia City and offer to help him.

Slocum smiled crookedly and started back down the hill when his foot slipped from under him. He caught himself with one hand, then recoiled. Sitting heavily, Slocum looked at his hand and then at the silver concho that had made an imprint in his flesh. He picked up the decoration and held it up high. The flash from it matched that he had seen earlier.

"The sun caught it just right," he decided. No one had been here—not today, but someone had left it, and that person was undoubtedly the same as the one who had spoken so furtively with Arly Penks.

Turning it over and over in his hand, Slocum remembered where he had seen similar decorations lately.

"Maybe you were something more than a damnfool gunman," Slocum said before tucking the concho into his shirt pocket. But what had gone on between Penks and the gunman that involved Slocum? That was a question he couldn't answer.

Right now, he had to get Cara back to town and do something about replacing the deed to the mine before real claim jumpers rode in.

"Mind looking after my gear for a spell?" asked Slocum. "I don't have any place to store it, except with the wagon and jackass at the stable."

"I would be happy to do so, John." Cara smiled brightly. "It insures that you will have to see me again."

"Wouldn't have it any other way," Slocum said. He watched as she made her way into the hotel, carrying his saddlebags, the oilcloth-wrapped six-shooter securely hidden in one bag. Slocum had been a drifter ever since the war and had sometimes owned less in the way of possessions than a six-shooter and a set of saddlebags, but somehow he felt a rising anger this time that some sneak thief had stolen everything else he owned from the shack.

He was rich. He owned a mine with enough silver in it to keep him living in high style the rest of his life. And yet sneak thieves made off with his saddle and other belongings.

The sun sank behind the tall mountains and turned Virginia City chilly again. Slocum had spent the entire day riding in the wagon, and his rear ached. He would have to find a good saddle horse and get back to riding, but first he wanted to establish his right to the Silver Jackass.

He had left the county registrar poking through the ruins of the land office, but the man had long since gone. Asking of the people walking down the street to gawk at the burned-out buildings, Slocum found that the registrar, and most other men, were at the Moose Hall for a volunteer fire company meeting.

The lure of the saloons caused Slocum to slow his pace, but he needed assurance he would not be done out of the mine more than he did a drink. And he began to regret leaving his six-shooter with Cara Penks. He pressed his finger into his shirt pocket and traced the outline of the silver concho there. If he ran into the gunman again, he wanted to be carrying his ebony-handled Colt Navy.

Yellow light streamed from the open doors of the Moose Hall, and Slocum followed the loud noise up the steps. He peered into the smoke-filled room and saw the familiar face of the Monumental Engine Company No. 6 captain on a stage with three men who were obviously politicians.

"We want to thank you, Captain Chambers, for your company's fine work this past week. You prevented an underground fire from turning into a real disaster—"

From the front row Slocum heard one of the miners he and Happy Harry had saved, the one named McDermont, call, "Three cheers for the volunteer firemen!"

The politician looked pained that he had been interrupted, but went along with the mass approval for Chambers and his men. Then he puffed out his chest until his vest buttons threatened to pop and continued, "We are appropriating even more money so you can continue your fine work. You and the other volunteer departments in Virginia City have worked diligently and well, and I—"

Slocum turned from the door and scanned the crowd until he found the registrar sitting at one side of the room. He pushed through the crowd until he sat beside the land agent.

"You again? You ought to be up there. Maybe you could shut that gasbag up."

"I've seen too many politicians tooting their own horn to believe I could ever get a word in edgewise," Slocum said. For a reply he got a broad smile.

"What you needin', son? You find your partners' deeds?"

"Gone," Slocum said, not wanting to elaborate. "I need to make sure there's no confusion over the claim, what with both my partners being dead."

"You got your deed? The one you showed me before?" The registrar pulled eyeglasses from his pocket and perched them on the end of his nose. He peered down at the soaked yellow sheet Slocum pulled from his pocket. With deliberate care he unfolded the sheet. It fell to pieces.

"Ink's too smeared to make anything out," the man said. "My advice stands. Get yourself on up to Carson City and get a copy. There's nuthin' I can do for you."

"What if someone turns up with a good copy and tries to sell the mine?"

"You mean somebody up and stole the other copies?" The registrar shook his head. "You and Happy Harry are too well known in town for that to happen. If I hear anything like that is happening—and all transactions go through my hands—I won't put up with it. Hell, Slocum,

you're a hero. You ought to go on up there and get the
mayor off the stage.''

''Thanks,'' Slocum said, tucking the useless deed back
into his pocket. He wasn't sure why he kept the deed except
as a reminder of what he truly owned. The Silver Jackass
was his—his and Cara Penks's.

Slocum stepped back into the clear night and sucked in
a deep breath to get the stale cigarette smoke hanging in
the Moose Lodge from his lungs. For a moment he couldn't
tell what put him on guard. Then he knew. A flash of light
reflecting off silver came from across the street in the
mouth of an alley.

Rather than walk down the steps of the Moose Lodge
Hall, Slocum vaulted the railing and landed lightly to one
side. In a crouch, he made his way to the side of the building. A dozen horses were tethered there. They stirred restlessly as he made his way through them. When he reached
the back of the lodge hall, he looked up and down the
street. Fewer stirred this night because of the volunteer fire
meeting and the political speeches being made, but enough
folks strolled about to assure Slocum he wasn't in a deserted town.

Somehow, the notion of people around him proved comforting. Usually Slocum preferred being alone and left to
his own devices. His hand returned to his shirt pocket and
the concho. He glanced over his shoulder to see if anyone
trailed him. Slocum didn't see anyone, but the feeling of
eyes watching him increased his uneasiness.

He stopped in the middle of the street and waited to see
if his unseen tracker would betray his position. Of all the
people Slocum saw, none appeared the least bit interested
in him. Moving slowly, he went into the saloon on his right.
Moving quickly once he reached the door to keep from
silhouetting himself too long, Slocum whipped inside. The
crush of heat from the gathered bodies and the stench of
stale beer and unwashed men hit him like a sledgehammer.

Normally, he would never have noticed, but tonight his

senses were honed to a sharp edge. Everything struck him and vied for his attention. The miners in the bar were mostly drunk and getting drunker. Two tried to fight at one side of the saloon. A huge haymaker missed its target by a country mile. The miner fell into his intended victim's arms, the pair of them falling to the floor laughing uproariously. Card games went on, the black-dressed gamblers systematically fleecing those intrepid enough to sit at their tables. And from the rear, Slocum saw a woman dressed in a torn, filthy red satin dress motioning to him in what she thought was a seductive fashion.

"Come on out, you big hunk," she called. "I got just what you want!"

Slocum fleetingly compared her coarse look and wanton dress with Cara Penks. It wasn't that he hadn't partaken of what women such as this one offered. He just had something better waiting for him now. He wished he could shake the feeling of impending disaster.

Again he regretted not strapping on his cross-draw holster and settling the comforting weight of his six-shooter at his left hip.

Slocum crossed the crowded saloon in six strides. The woman smiled, a black, broken tooth showing as she thought she was going to strike it rich.

"You are a big one," she said, reaching for Slocum with a filthy hand sporting cracked fingernails. "In a lot of ways, unless I miss the mark."

"Not tonight," Slocum said, shaking her hand off his shirt and crowding past her into the alley. To his left lay the cribs where the whores plied their trade. To the right opened the alley into the street in front of the saloon.

"Hey, you can't treat a lady like that!" she protested. "I got my dignity, you know."

From inside the saloon came a raucous roar of laughter. "That ain't all you got, Sarah. And you're real willin' to spread it around, too. Just ask ol' Nevada Pete what fell off from the clap after he paid a quarter to fuck you!"

Slocum hurried into the alleyway before the woman could answer the charge. If anyone trailed him, they might have been lured into the crowded saloon. It would take a few minutes to determine that Slocum was no longer inside. By then he could be back at Cara's hotel and retrieve his six-gun.

A wagon rattled past in the street. Slocum took the opportunity to cross behind it, using it as a shield from anyone spying on him from farther down the street. He never heard the gunshot that sent a slug flying smack into his chest.

9

Slocum wondered if this was what it felt like to be dead. Every move he made sent new ripples of pain into his chest. Each breath filled him with liquid fire, but rolling to his side proved worse. The pain pulled a black curtain across his vision for a moment, but it left the agony. Realizing the pain was never going to leave, seeing or not, Slocum struggled to get his hands and knees under him.

The new flood of pain cleared his senses enough for him to know he wasn't dead. This filled him with a mixture of determination and all-consuming anger at the man who had tried to dry-gulch him. Slocum had known someone had been stalking him, and he had tried to avoid him, but his pursuer had been too cunning.

''Rifle,'' grunted Slocum, falling facedown into the dirt. No one came to his side. Slocum worried that he had turned invisible, then realized he was pitched up against the board-walk at the side of the street away from probing eyes. ''He bushwhacked me using a rifle. Wouldn't even come up and face me.''

Somehow, knowing how his attacker had shot him angered Slocum enough to sit up. Slocum's hand moved to

his heart where the bullet had entered his chest. He expected to find a hole going straight through his body, but
his fingers only came away with sticky blood. Blood and
silver dust.

Fumbling in his shirt pocket, Slocum winced with new
pain as he pulled out the thick silver concho. The metal
had been bent almost double by the passage of the bullet.
The shot had glanced along the concho and deflected
enough to save his life. Pulling open his shirt revealed the
bloody streak and how bits of silver from the ornament had
entered his flesh.

Slocum tried to pluck out slivers of the silver but found
his hand was shaking too badly. He pushed to his feet and
immediately sat back down, his legs too weak to hold him.
He drew in a slow, deep breath and let his strength return.
Then he walked on rubbery legs down the street in the
direction he had intended before being bushwhacked.

At Cara's hotel he didn't go through the lobby, knowing
he would have to answer too many questions. Instead, he
found the side stairs and painfully made his way up them
to the door on the second floor. It was locked, but Slocum's
persistence forced it open. He took only two steps before
he collapsed—into Cara's arms.

The two of them almost crashed to the floor, but the
dark-haired woman braced herself against the wall and held
him upright long enough for him to regain his balance.

"Evening, Cara," he said.

"John! You've been shot! Whatever happened?"

"Don't want to talk about it in the hallway. The room
clerk might get nosy."

"Gracious," she said, shaking her head as if a small
child had tracked mud across her freshly swept kitchen
floor. Cara guided him into the door she had just opened
and let him fall onto the bed. Slocum rolled to his side to
keep from getting blood onto the bedspread, then realized
it was too late.

"You *were* shot, weren't you? This is not the type of

wound I would have thought, though I have no experience with such an injury.''

She bent close and peered at his chest with its oozing wound. Slocum saw her shake her head, raven hair spilling down.

''I declare, there is *silver* in the wound! Did someone shoot you with a silver bullet? I've never heard of such a thing.''

Slocum had, but didn't bother telling her what had to be hunted that way. ''This saved my life.'' He pulled the bent concho from his pocket and handed it to Cara. She turned it over in her hand and shook her head again.

''An angel rides on your shoulder, John Slocum. From what you say, this ought to have killed you. Instead, it merely grazed you.''

''I wouldn't call it 'mere,' '' Slocum said. His ribs had started to ache rather than hurt now. ''Can you get it cleaned up a mite? I've got some work to do.'' His eyes went to the saddlebags with his Colt Navy in them resting on the small marble-topped table at one side of the room.

''I spend more time bandaging you than I do talking with you,'' Cara complained as she went about pulling out clean bandages unused from the last time she had patched up Slocum.

He said nothing as she picked at the bits of silver buried in his chest with a pair of tweezers. He concentrated on what he would do to the gunman with the silver conchos when he caught up with him. The only dilemma Slocum had was whether to kill the man outright or try to find what his business with Arly Penks had been before killing him.

Curiosity was a powerful drug that worked its way into his body and mind. Slocum wanted to know what had gone on between the men, but revenge burned brighter still. The feel of his finger coming back on the trigger that would send forth the slug—

''John. John!'' Cara's voice brought him out of his vision of facing the gunfighter and removing him once and for all time.

"Sorry. I was thinking of something else."

"You always seem to think of things other than me," she said in a low voice. "Why is that? Don't you find me attractive? Or don't you believe in falling in love with your nurse?"

Slocum laughed, then gasped when Cara's hands worked on the mound in his pants. His laughter died as his green eyes locked with her bright blue ones. She was right about always doctoring him but dead wrong that he didn't find her beautiful.

"You're about the loveliest vision I've ever seen," Slocum said in a voice matching hers.

"The wound does not bother you too much, does it? If not, I know some medicine that might perk you right up." Her hand continued to massage his crotch. Slocum felt life stirring there as he grew harder. Cara felt it, too, and started gripping with more fervor. Then she struggled to pull open the buttons holding his pants on.

She skinned Slocum from his pants in the wink of an eye and had his erection firmly clutched in her hand, moving up and down slowly. He sighed with every trip from the thick base to the sensitive tip.

"I don't know if I can take much of that. You are drawing all life out of me," he said.

"Then let me put some back in." Cara tossed her head and sent her long black hair flying over one shoulder. She bent forward, and her eager lips fixed on the very tip of his manhood. Her tongue rolled around a mite, then worked down the sensitive underside.

Shivers of desire passed through Slocum's body. Minutes earlier he had been feeling half past dead. His chest ached and his back bothered him. Now all he could think of was the marvel of the gorgeous woman's mouth moving all over him.

As suddenly as she had begun, Cara drew back. Cool

wind from the window blew across his saliva-coated erection and sent new chills into his body.

"Cold, it's turning cold," he cautioned. "You wouldn't want that, would you?"

"Then we must put it somewhere that will be warm," she said, hiking her skirts. Cara straddled his waist and did a shimmy that made her breasts bob and dance under her blouse. Slocum reached up and clutched them, not caring if his dirty hands left prints on her starched white front. Beneath the crisp fabric he felt her nipples hardening with lust for him.

As Cara moved above him, he felt the tip of his manhood brush across the tangled mat of her sex. Then he was pulled entirely into soft warmth that clutched at him like a hand in a velvet glove. Slocum gasped again as she took his full length into her and began twisting her hips slightly from side to side.

He opened his eyes and saw the look of stark delight on her lovely face. Cara's eyes were closed and her face was turned up as she worked her hips up and down slightly.

His hands gripped her breasts more tightly. He felt the quickening of her heartbeat, the way her breathing sped up, and even the flow of life within her as it animated her. Color flushed her neck and shoulders and Cara began to pant as her desire mounted.

"You're about the best thing that's happened to me since I came to Virginia City," Cara said, looking down at him, her eyes glazed with lust. "Nothing has gone right, nobody has cared, Arlin is dead. But you, John, you're so full of life."

His hands left the hidden mounds buried under he blouse and moved down to her slender waist. He could almost circle that trim middle with his hands. He tightened his grip and urged her to lift more than she was off his body. He felt himself slipping from her moist interior. It took an act of supreme self-control to push her up and away, but then it was all worth it when he relaxed.

Her body crashed down and he sank deep into her again. They both gasped at the sudden intrusion.

"We're going to be rich, Cara," he said to her. "The two of us together."

"We're rich now," she said, gasping with pleasure. "We have one another. What else can there be?"

Before Slocum could answer, she rose and fell again, this time grinding her hips into his with more power. He was still weak from being shot and could hardly move—and he had no desire to. Letting the beautiful young woman set the pace suited him just fine. The pressures mounting in his loins were controllable—for the moment—and he reveled in every movement she made.

Side to side, up and down, Cara Penks moved with increasing urgency. Slocum's hands tightened around her waist as he pushed her up and pulled her down onto him. The added power made the lovemaking all the more intense. But the feel of her female flesh totally surrounding him slowly eroded his control. His balls began to pulse and throb as the white-hot tide threatened to spew forth.

"Faster," he gasped out to the woman. "Move, move!"

"Yes, yes, John, yes!" she cried. Her hips flew like a shuttlecock. Each downward plunge Cara tried to take more of him into her yielding body. And then she arched her back and cried out in wanton desire.

Slocum was no longer able to withstand the erotic pressures she placed upon him. He spilled his seed, lifting off the bed as he tried to split her apart. They strove together for a long, glorious moment and then sagged back to the bed, sweating and tired from their efforts.

"John, that was so . . . so special," she finished lamely. "I haven't much experience in these matters, but I rather enjoyed that." She smiled almost shyly at him as if she needed reassurance that she had done well.

"You plumb wore me out. Never been this good, Cara," he told her, and it wasn't much of a lie. "And I can attest

I never had a nurse who could tend me as good as you do.''

Cara Penks snuggled into the hollow of his shoulder, the scent of her hair rising to his nostrils. They lay together for a spell, then Slocum's gaze drifted toward the table and his saddlebags. He moved her to one side and stood.

''John, what are you doing?''

''This was pleasant, Cara, and I ought to spend the rest of the night here, but I have business to tend to.'' He opened the saddlebags and took out the oilcloth package. Unwrapping it quickly revealed his Colt Navy. He spun the cylinder and saw that it carried six charges. He bent to pick up his pants.

''John, what are you going to do?''

''I know who ambushed me. If I don't get him first, he'll try again the next time he sees me. I have the advantage now, if he thinks I am dead.''

He settled into his jeans and then pulled on his bloodied shirt. He looked a fright, but it hardly mattered. Killing a man didn't require Sunday go-to-meeting duds.

''Do you know how to use that? I didn't know you even had a pistol, John.'' Cara sat up in bed, hugging herself as if she had a chill.

''I know how to use this,'' Slocum said. The way he strapped on his holster and settled the ebony-handled Colt showed years of practice. He touched the butt, made sure the six-shooter rested easy, and then walked to the door.

''I'll be back when it's over,'' he told her.

''No, no you won't,'' she said in a choked voice.

''You don't want to see me again?'' Slocum halfway expected this reaction. Cara Penks was a cultured woman who had discovered she had made love to a Western barbarian. He didn't much blame her, though leaving her hurt a mite more than he had thought it would.

''All the men in my life abandon me. Father, Arlin, Matthew—'' She bit her lip and turned away.

Slocum didn't ask who Matthew might be. He had no

right to pry into Cara's life. If he had been a betrothed who had either died or left her, that explained how she had come to be so good when it came to pleasuring a man.

"I'll be back, if you'll see me."

"I will—if you're still alive. John, whoever tried to kill you is a murderer!" Cara leaned back when she saw the expression on his face. John Slocum had ridden with William Quantrill and had done his share of killing then. And after the war, he had not led an easy life. Any man crossing him had died, some fast, some slowly—but all his enemies were six feet under.

The black-dressed shootist would be another left in an unmarked grave out in the Virginia City potter's field.

"Get some rest," Slocum advised. "We can talk when I get back." With that he turned and left the hotel room. As he closed the door, he thought he heard Cara crying softly. He tried to forget it. She worried that he would end up facedown in the street. It wouldn't be like that. Not now.

Feeling better with the weight of his six-gun at his side, Slocum went down the stairs and into the cold Nevada night. His step lengthened and he felt power returning to his body. No man tried to dry-gulch him and lived to brag on it. No one.

Slocum stepped into the saloon where he had felt the eyes on his back and scanned the crowd for the gunman sporting the conchos and the huge silver belt buckle. The din died when the miners inside spotted Slocum and his wide stance. They knew a man ready to kill when they saw one. But Slocum ducked back outside.

The man he sought had not been inside. One by one he checked the saloons along D Street. Those on F Street yielded no sign of his quarry, either. But Slocum was not going to give up. If word got around that he was still alive and looking for the back-shooting son of a bitch, he would have to sleep with his eyes open. Worse, not killing the gunman right away put Cara in danger.

Slocum had seen cowards before and knew they thought

nothing of striking at him through a woman.

Another ten saloons passed his scrutiny, and still there was no trace of the gunman. Slocum felt no anticipation, no pressure of time, though. A deadly killing coldness had settled on him. Eventually, he would discover the man's lair, and when he did, lead would fly.

One of them would walk away. This time it would be John Slocum.

He came back to the saloon near the site of the fire the night before, the first place he had encountered the gunman. But Slocum again came up empty-handed. The barkeep had not seen the gunman—or lied well enough to convince Slocum—and none knew the man's name.

Slocum went back into the street and pondered where to search next when he heard an all-too-familiar sound carried on the wind.

The fire alarm bell rang with such insistence that Slocum walked to the next intersection and looked uphill toward the town of Gold Hill slipping over the divide. Flames fifty feet high rose from the houses there. Another deadly fire threatened to rage through the tinderbox-dry town.

He had to jump out of the way as the Monumental Engine Company raced past, some firemen still struggling into their red shirts and leather helmets. The rest of the town stirred and came alive, making it even harder for Slocum to find the gunman.

Or perhaps it would become easier to find his quarry. Slocum turned toward the fire and followed the volunteers up the hill, still intent on having it out with the bushwhacking scoundrel.

10

Like a freshet that becomes a stream and the stream that
then flows into a river, so did the miners in Virginia City
rush to the fire. A few trickled from the saloons and
pointed. These few who rushed to watch were joined by an
ever increasing number, until Slocum was sure no one
would remain behind. That convinced him he ought to go
along. If the gunman he sought was anywhere in town, it
was probably going to be where the majority of the people
were.

After all, the gunslinger thought he had killed Slocum
and had no reason to hightail it from the Comstock. If anything, he would be strutting about and bragging to any who
would listen how he had just killed Slocum.

"This is a bad one," a man called to a friend, still struggling into his pants as he came from a small house along
the road. "All Gold Hill is going up this time."

"Will it spread?" The man dropped to the ground and
kicked hard to get into his pants. Then he tucked in his
nightshirt as he came to his feet. "I ain't gonna leave Bess
and the kids if it comes down the hill into Virginia City."

Slocum saw the man's concern. The flames devouring

the buildings in Gold Hill rose even higher than before, coming over the divide and turning the night into an eerie, deadly day. This was a fire that threatened everyone and everything in its path.

"All the fire companies are turning out. Don't worry none. They'll stop it before it gets out of control. I think I can hear someone calling 'First water!' right now."

Slocum hurried on, noting that no one believed the firemen were going to control this blaze easily. He began to pant from exertion when he hit a steep stretch of road leading to the houses over the divide in Gold Hill. The richest of the rich in the Comstock district lived there. While they were best able to sustain loss, Slocum hated to see anyone burned out of his home. And the danger to the people mounted with every passing minute as the fire jumped from one house to its neighbor.

"You gonna help out, Slocum?" called a man struggling into a red shirt and making his way up the steep hill next to Slocum. "We kin use every hand, and Cap'n Chambers says you got the touch when it comes to making the steam engine work."

"Chambers's son is the one saying that," Slocum returned. The boy had taken quite a shine to Slocum and still regaled all and sundry with tales of Slocum's expertise. Slocum held back and let the volunteer pass him on the way to the struggle. The minute the man moved away from him, Slocum tugged at the brim of his Stetson and pulled it down to protect his face. Hot wind gusted from the direction of the fire and promised blisters if he pressed on.

But Slocum did. He fought to pull his eyes away from the mesmerizing dance of the leaping flames and studied the crowd that had gathered to watch the firemen. Most were only half dressed and still rubbing sleep from their eyes, pulled from their beds by the strident clangor of the alarm bells. But some had come directly from the saloons in Virginia City, fully dressed and awake.

"Hey, mister, wanta place a little wager?" asked a skeletally thin gambler. Slocum saw how he rolled a silver dollar up and down between his fingers on one hand to show his dexterity. Or perhaps it was an unconscious move.

"On what?" Slocum asked, trying to spot the gunman and irritated that he was being detained.

"Can they stop the fire 'fore it gets to Virginia City? And if not, how much of Virginia City will get burned to the ground?"

"You're betting on something like that? Which side are you taking? What odds?"

The moment of hesitation told Slocum it didn't matter to the gambler how he bet or what odds he gave. The man would lay off the bet to someone else so he collected a small transaction fee regardless of the wager. The gambler won and everyone else lost.

"Maybe it would be best if you took your turn helping the firemen," Slocum said, his hand drifting toward his six-gun. "They can use someone to haul the hose carriages up that steep hill and do some of the harder work so they can worry about putting out the fire. It seems to me that you've been thinking too much and not working enough." Slocum almost laughed as the gambler stepped away and then faded into the fringe of the crowd.

He was always amazed at the number of people willing to make a dollar off someone else's misery. Men, women, and children might be dying in this uncontrollable fire. Even if they didn't, their belongings would be destroyed completely. Slocum wondered if it had occurred to the greedy gambler that money might be had by betting on how many would die this night.

An unexpected explosion almost knocked him to the ground. Slocum swung about and threw up his arm to protect his face as a heated gust carrying burning debris shot past. Whatever had been stored in an outbuilding had gone up with impressive violence. Worse, it caused the fire to spread even faster.

Torn between joining the volunteers in their battle and

continuing his hunt for the man who had tried to kill him, Slocum slipped along the edge of the crowd. The chuffing of the new steam pump and the loud cries from the men toiling to hold back the wall of flames convinced Slocum he would only be in the way if he joined them. This wasn't a simple fire to be put out by just anyone. Experts had to work with diligence and skill to keep from making the fire worse as it chewed through one building after another in Gold Hill.

Not paying attention to where he walked, Slocum bumped into a man and recoiled. The sheriff's badge shining on the man's vest caused Slocum to back off. Sheriff Tyler hardly noticed. He was too busy talking with a small, sooty-faced man wearing a volunteer's red shirt. The fireman waved his arms like a windmill gone berserk and coughed now and again, but a snippet of his tirade caught Slocum's attention. He stayed close behind the sheriff, eavesdropping on the conversation.

"I *know* it was, Tyler. I seen enough fires to know."

"That's a mighty serious charge, Jerry," the sheriff said.

"No doubt in my mind. None at all. The way the fire started shows someone set it. The fire goes straight up the walls real fast-like and gets into places it doesn't, otherwise. Most fires starting from piles of filthy rags smolder for a while, smoke a lot, and then reluctantly start to burn. Not this one. This one exploded, *whoosh!*" The fireman turned and stabbed a dirty finger toward one ruined house fifty yards away. "That there's the place. You can smell kerosene all over the walls, if that's any more proof for you."

"What if someone tipped over a kerosene lamp?" Slocum asked, his mind working in a dozen different ways with this information.

"Amounts," the fireman said positively. "There's just not much oil in a single lamp. It might start the fire, but it doesn't soak everything through and through. It takes a *lot* of kerosene to make an odor linger after a hot, long-burning fire."

"Just like the fire in Doc's office," Tyler mused, rubbing his stubbly chin. This caught Slocum's attention even more.

"You saying the fire in Doc Hanley's office was arson?" Slocum asked. The sheriff glanced over his shoulder, irritated at the interruption.

"I've seen you around. Slocum, ain't it? Well, Slocum, you just go on and join in the fun watching Gold Hill burn to the ground. This don't concern you none." Sheriff Tyler coldly glared at him until Slocum backed off. He had no reason to rile the lawman, but what the volunteer fireman said about the fire being set held Slocum's attention.

He couldn't keep from turning it over and over in his head. Happy Harry might have been murdered rather than the innocent victim of an unavoidable fire. Slocum waited for the sheriff to depart before sauntering over to the fireman.

"What do you want? I got to get back," the man said, but he showed no real interest in continuing the thankless battle against the consuming tongues of flame leaping from one house to another.

"What do you look for in a fire that's been set?"

The fireman shrugged. "Over there, one spot was hotter than the others. Burned quick, didn't leave much behind. When it burns slower, cooler, charring on the timbers is plain as the nose on your face. And the smell. Always check for the odor of kerosene." He tapped the side of his sizable nose and then began the trek up the hill to rejoin his volunteer unit.

Slocum passed through the crowd one last time in his hunt for the gunman but didn't spot him. Somehow, his footsteps took him back to an almost deserted Virginia City and the burned-out husk of Doc Hanley's office. On the way, Slocum stopped in front of the land office and just stared at the ruins for a moment.

The sheriff had said the fire in Doc Hanley's office had been set, but what about this fire? Slocum remembered how a secondary explosion had come from the land office. He had thought it was the file cabinets feeding the blaze, but now he wondered. The cabinets had been emptied and the contents strewn about. To help speed the fire along?

That seemed an increasingly likely answer. Walking into the ruins, Slocum tried to figure out where the kerosene might have been splashed, using the fireman's hints about arson fires. The heat had been too intense everywhere, fed by the mountains of loose paper. Slocum could guess, but he didn't know exactly what to look for. He decided to go two doors down and see what he could piece together in the doctor's devastated office.

Poking about, Slocum found an area at the rear of the office that had simply vanished. Picking up wood near this area, Slocum sniffed hard, trying to detect the familiar odor of kerosene. His nostrils flared when he found it.

"Who's there?" came a sudden question. "Put your hands up and come out where I can see you."

Slocum rose and turned to face Doc Hanley. The physician lowered an old double-barreled shotgun when he recognized Slocum.

"What you doing here, son?" he asked. "Can't get enough of the fire? Go on up to Gold Hill and see what's happening there."

"Why aren't you there? I'm certain there will be people injured."

"Gold Hill's got its own doctor. And I've been real busy." Hanley put the butt of the shotgun on the floor and leaned on the muzzle. Seeing Slocum's expression when he did this, Hanley shook his head and laughed without much humor. "The gun's not loaded. I heal, I don't kill. Fact is, I got more patients than I can handle now, so I don't even have to go and wound them myself anymore."

Slocum had heard the edge in Hanley's voice when he had declared how busy he had been. Slocum inquired.

"Reckon we're both coming around to the same conclusion. What did you find?"

"I poked around at the land registrar's office," Slocum

said carefully. ''Seems to me there was more to the fire than can be laid on the doorstep of pure accident.''

''What did you find there? The same as you did here?'' pressed Hanley. He pointed to the eaten away section of his office wall.

''Hard to tell, but I'd be willing to bet money I found traces of kerosene, both here and over at the land office.''

''That goes along with what I found in your partner,'' Hanley said. He sank down on his haunches, using the shotgun as support. The doctor looked up at Slocum. ''Don't go flying off the handle, son. I haven't had a chance to tell Sheriff Tyler about this yet, and I will. You got to promise to let him deal with this.''

''Happy Harry was killed,'' Slocum said flatly. ''That's obvious. He was laid up with a broken leg and someone set fire to your office.''

To Slocum's surprise, the physician shook his head sadly. ''Not like that, son. Not at all. Harry Harlan carried a slug in him. From the burned body it was hard to prove it killed him outright, but he wasn't going anywhere.''

''Tell me,'' Slocum said, his voice carrying the steel edge of command honed from years in the army.

''His spine was shattered. No amount of burning could hide that. I dallied about and found a lead slug buried in his backbone. The way I see it, somebody came into the back room, shot him, and then set the fire to cover the crime.''

Slocum's hands clenched, then relaxed only after he forced them to.

''So he didn't burn to death. That's a terrible way to die.''

''Son, there's no good way to die if you're not inclined to kick the bucket. Happy Harry had years and years left in that old body of his.'' Doc Hanley heaved to his feet and stared at Slocum. ''Don't go doing anything illegal. Let catching the devil who did all this lay on the sheriff's shoulders.''

Slocum only nodded. He couldn't know for certain, but he thought he knew who had killed Happy Harry, and who the arsonist was who had set fire to the land office and Doc Hanley's office, and who it was who had tried to dry-gulch him only hours earlier.

The black-dressed gunman with the silver conchos and bright belt buckle seemed perfect to hang all the crimes on. Only one question burned as brightly in Slocum's mind as the fire still raging up in Gold Hill: Why? What did the shootist get out of the fires and killing Slocum and Harry Harlan?

11

The heat from the Gold Hill fire washed through Virginia City and made Slocum sweat rivers as he walked along B Street. He hardly noticed, since he was so deep in thought. Hearing that Happy Harry had been murdered before the fire changed everything in his life. He still hunted for the conch-wearing gunman, but now Slocum wasn't as likely to cut him down where he stood.

Not until the man answered some hard questions.

"Did he kill Happy Harry and then want me out of the way?" Slocum asked himself. A gust of wind carrying a blinding cloud of dust, smoke, and soot was his only answer. Other questions rose. Maybe Arly Penks had set the powder properly but had died in some other fashion. Slocum wasn't sure how he might have done it, but the mysterious gunfighter could have killed Penks, too. The day he and Happy Harry had thought they had watched Penks high on the mountainside came back. A flash of silver. Off conchos? Had Penks known the gunslinger?

The Silver Jackass Mine was the obvious goal for someone killing off the three partners, but how did the gunman intend to profit? If the man was a claim jumper, he was going to a lot of trouble. Most jumpers simply moved within rifle range, pot-shot the owners, then moved in after disposing of the bodies.

Slocum's hand touched the spot where the bullet had torn apart the silver concho. He might have hit on the truth of the matter, though it seemed the shootist was going out of his way to do something others did with more dispatch.

And why set fire to the registrar's office? If he intended to jump the claim, the concho-decorated shootist would have forged sales contracts. In the bustle of everyday life in Virginia City, nobody much cared who pulled ore from the ground. There was more than enough to go around for everyone.

The sun crept over the jagged edge of the mountains and shone in Slocum's eyes. He found himself walking slowly toward the funeral parlor down the street from Doc Hanley's office. For a moment, Slocum wasn't sure what brought him there. Then he came to a decision about how to find the gunman and his reasons for such senselessly murderous ways.

As the undertaker opened the front door for another day's business, Slocum went inside. The man straightened as he eyed Slocum and his tattered clothing, but the man's watery eyes came to rest on the well-used Colt Navy secured at his left hip.

"How may I help you, sir? I am Arthur Conroy, funeral director for our fine town." The undertaker's voice grated like glass on metal.

"Harry Harlan—Happy Harry—you have him waiting for burial?"

"Sadly, yes, I do. Such a decent fellow. A pity he had to pass on at such a young age." Conroy tented his fingers in front of him, as if imitating the chapel over on E and Taylor streets. Slocum struggled to remember what the white-steepled church's name was. Then he remembered. Saint Mary's in the Mountains.

Slocum had never thought of Happy Harry as being young. "How old was he?"

"Why, I cannot say exactly. Perhaps forty. For many this is a ripe old age, but for Mr. Harlan, it was hardly a start. His father lived to be more than seventy."

"Harry was from around here?"

"No, not at all. I came to Virginia City a few years back from Sacramento. I knew Mr. Harlan's family there. It was a pleasant surprise finding an old acquaintance already here. I assure you, I will do my best work with the deceased. He was a good man." Conroy smiled, but it was all in his lips. There was no real pleasure of remembrance anywhere else in the man's countenance.

Slocum doubted he would find anyone who knew Happy Harry better than the man who was going to plant him six feet under. He worried the questions that needed answering until they came out all in one.

"Who'd want Harry dead? Did he have any enemies, men who threatened him?"

"Why, I know of no one. Mr. Harlan was well liked, a generous man with his money. He often bought drinks for the others and, ahem, furnished fodder for my business."

"How's that?"

"Many in this town drink themselves to an early end. Sometimes, they become intemperate and shoot one another. Mr. Harlan's generosity furthered these unseemly ends." Now Conroy's smile turned genuine. Slocum wished it had remained insincere.

"But nobody held a grudge against Harry?" Slocum frowned. He had known Harry Harlan for only a few months, but the man's good-natured joshing had turned aside many insults and kept them working together when Slocum might have simply ridden on.

"I know of no one. He was generous with his money in other ways. He reputedly loaned money lavishly, when he had it. Seldom do I remember hearing of anyone repaying, nor did it much bother Mr. Harlan. You were one of his partners, weren't you?''

Slocum nodded, thinking hard.

"Did you ever hear Arly Penks say anything against Happy Harry?''

"Ah, the other partner, the one so unfortunately lost in your mine explosion." Seeing Slocum's surprise at his knowledge, Arthur Conroy smiled even more broadly. He looked like a death's head, and Slocum wished he would return to his more usual somber expression of mock grief. "It is my business to know of deaths. With no body to bury, well—" The undertaker shrugged.

"Penks might deserve a memorial service," Slocum said. "I remember such things from the war.''

"Ah, yes. So many died, the pieces scattered to the four winds in bloody slaughter. You are willing to combine their ceremonies?'' The undertaker rubbed his hands together at the notion of profiting from Penks's death after all.

"Might be. Have to ask his kin," Slocum said.

"I was unaware of any relatives. Truth to tell, I never even met Mr. Penks.''

"A sister," Slocum supplied. "What about Happy Harry's family over in Sacramento?''

"Alas, they are all deceased. They died just before I moved to Virginia City. Since these matters are not taken lightly by my staff or me, when might I know the type of ceremonial service to best provide for Mr. Penks's eternal rest?''

"I'll let you know soon. The same with Happy Harry. Thanks for your help.'' Slocum wheeled about and left the funeral parlor fast, suddenly glad to be in the open air once more. The walls had closed in around him, but now he had only the blue sky above and the walls of mountains around him. He hardly noticed the town just coming to life.

Having found out nothing to help concerning Happy Harry, Slocum turned toward the International Hotel where Cara stayed. He hesitated going to her again after their last parting. He was never quite certain what Cara wanted from him—or what he expected from her. She was a woman of surprising moods—and lovely, so heartachingly lovely.

"Oh, John, I was just coming to find you," Cara Penks said, coming from the hotel lobby as Slocum reached the bottom step leading to the boardwalk. "Have you eaten breakfast yet?"

"No, can't say that I have." Slocum's belly rumbled at the mention of food. He had never known steady meals, but it seemed since he had struck it rich at the Silver Jackass, he was eating less than ever.

"Join me, will you?" Her blue eyes locked with his green ones, challenging him to deny her this small triumph of the will. He wasn't going to hinder her desire to buy him another meal, even if he ended up paying for it.

"Wearing this doesn't bother you, does it?" He patted the holster holding his six-shooter.

"It does, but many others out West wear such weapons. It is expected in some circles. I shall learn to live with it, if not accept it."

"Good," Slocum said, extending his arm for her to take. Cara's touch was light at first, then she squeezed down harder to bring back memories of their more intimate moments together. "I've got a few questions that need answering."

"About Arlin? I know so little of him. He left when I was young, you remember."

"So you said. What was in the letter he sent your pa? Did he mention anything about friends or enemies? Men who might have had it in for him?"

"Father never revealed the contents of the letter to me. Only that he was extremely distraught and disappointed with Arlin. From this I thought he meant that Arlin had run afoul of the law."

They entered the café, Slocum touching the brim of his Stetson in greeting to the amiable owner. As before, the service was quick and the food good. After a few minutes of silently chewing on his steak, Slocum asked, "What kind of trouble had Arly gotten into before he left Philadelphia?"

"Why, I—" Cara flushed and bit her lower lip. Her eyes dropped to her plate and she pushed her food around aimlessly. The question had flustered her more than Slocum thought it should.

"He kill somebody?"

"No, nothing like that. I heard rumors later, after he left, only vicious lies, I am sure, how Arlin had been stealing from our neighbors."

"He'd break in and swipe the family silver?" Slocum doubted that was exactly the crime, but it wasn't anything he would have put past Arly Penks. The man had never seemed square to him, no matter how loudly Happy Harry had vouched for him. From the little Slocum had learned of Harry Harlan, the man never thought ill of anyone and probably had been taken in by Penks's tall tales.

"Rumors, nothing more. Still, he left under a cloud of suspicion," Cara said in a choked voice. "But he is— was—my only relative."

"Whatever he might have done elsewhere, he left you his interest in the mine. That ought to account for something. When you go back to Philadelphia, you can lord it over those folks who said he'd never amount to anything." Slocum softened it as much as he could for the woman.

She looked up and shrugged. "It hardly matters after all this time," she said, but he heard in her tone how much it did matter to her. "Besides, I might stay here. As long as you are here, that is."

Slocum wondered at her motives. Was she only hanging on to him from desperation, from having her entire family killed off? He was a drifter and as hard to hold onto as a dust devil bouncing over the parched desert sands.

"I've got a bit of work to do at the mine. I want to clear away some of the debris from the collapse, sift through it, and get some decent samples to take to Carson City for assay, then make certain the claim is firm.'' Slocum finished his breakfast and sat back, watching Cara push her food from one side of the plate to the other. She had hardly eaten a mouthful. Slocum wondered what the burr was under her saddle.

''Do you mind if I accompany you to Carson City?''

''Not at all. If anything, it might help out when I talk to the state registrar of deeds. There shouldn't be any trouble, but if there is, you can vouch for me.'' Slocum reached across the table and put his hand on her arm. Her eyes rose to meet his. ''You don't have to worry about me cheating you out of your share in the mine. I reckon you deserve half.''

''That's too much, John. You deserve more. Only one-third, if anything at all, ought to come my way.''

''Because that was Arly's share?'' Slocum shook his head. ''I've done some inquiry and found that Happy Harry didn't have any family left. There might be a cousin or some such in Sacramento, but I doubt finding them would be possible. That makes the Silver Jackass all mine to do with as I see fit. And you get half.''

''You are such a fine man, John. A true Southern gentleman.'' Her hand covered his and there were no words possible for several heartbeats. Slocum got to feeling uncomfortable and pulled back.

''There are errands I have to run before getting on back to the mine,'' he said. He didn't tell Cara he still wanted to find the gunman and have it out with him. Only the black-clad, silver-concho-studded gunfighter held answers to serious questions.

''Should I prepare to leave by noon?'' Cara's question caught him by surprise.

''Reckon so, if you want to go out to the mine with me again. But you'd be hard-pressed to get back to town before dark.''

''There's no need for me to stay in the hotel, John. I saw

the cabin. There would be ample privacy there.'' She flashed him her shy-wanton smile and added, ''Privacy enough for the two of us.''

''The hotel's a sight more comfortable,'' Slocum said, not really wanting to talk her out of staying at the mine shack. ''But it would give us a head start getting to Carson City.''

''The matter is settled. Noon, in front of the hotel.'' For a moment, Cara Penks stared at him, then rose and quickly left. Slocum leaned back and watched her trim figure depart, wondering where this would lead. He didn't know, and it didn't much matter. He'd play the hand until winning the pot or losing everything. He had been busted before and the prospect didn't scare him. But winning this time would be a true delight.

Slocum paid with the last of his water-soaked greenbacks and left, deciding to make one last turn through the saloons in his search for the architect of his woes. After an hour of hunting, Slocum still hadn't found the gunman or anyone willing to admit having seen him. It was as if the man was a ghost and simply drifted in and out of Slocum's life. The only thing real about him was the bullet he had tried to put smack in Slocum's heart.

Giving up on his search, Slocum headed for the livery where he had left the wagon and jackass. He rounded the corner and started for the partially open barn door when he saw his quarry. The gunfighter stood with his back toward Slocum, but he was instantly recognizable. Sunlight flashed off the silver conchos studding his pants and hat.

Slocum's hand went to his Colt Navy, but he did not draw. The gunman shouted at someone inside the stable, and Slocum knew it wasn't the young boy who tended the animals. The tow-headed boy lounged in the shade some distance away, near the pile of hay meant for the horses in the stable.

''No!'' the gunslinger shouted. He waved his arms about wildly. Slocum pulled his six-shooter and cocked it. The gunman was too intent on his argument to notice.

Slocum almost caught sight of the man inside the stable, but the moving gunman and shadows kept him from real identification. The hidden man shouted something and shoved the shootist outside. The stable door slammed, cutting off the black-dressed gunfighter's retreat.

"You!" the gunman snarled. "How come you're still alive?"

"It takes more than a low-down rattler to kill me," Slocum said. His six-gun rose and his finger tightened. He didn't care if this was a fair fight. The gunman had tried to bushwhack him when he was unarmed. But the man's speed was blinding. He drew and got off a wild shot in Slocum's direction.

Slocum squeezed off his shot and felt the familiar recoil in his hand. But there was no sense of hitting his target. The shootist ducked and moved as if he might have been hit, but Slocum thought this might be a trick. He fired again and missed, blowing splinters off the stable wall.

The stable hand had been frozen until now. The boy shot to his feet and sped off, going for the law. Slocum knew he had only a few seconds before the town marshal or the sheriff came running up and denied him his revenge.

"Stop and fight, damn you!" yelled Slocum, firing again. He had three rounds left and he meant for all of them to end up in the gunman's worthless carcass. Running forward, he heard the thunder of hooves from the rear of the stable, but he knew the gunslinger hadn't mounted. That was the shadowy figure the shootist had argued with.

Slocum slowed his headlong run and turned cautious, wary of walking into another ambush. Men tended to use the same ploy over and over. If the man had tried to dry-gulch him once, he would do it again.

Spinning fast, Slocum came around the corner of the stable. His Colt Navy was leveled and ready to fire, but the gunfighter had vanished into thin air. Slocum hunted for long minutes trying to find him but knew it was time to leave when he heard the sheriff approaching with the yammering stable hand.

The jackass seemed almost happy to pull the wagon away from the gathering storm created by the law.

12

Slocum stripped off his shirt, peeling away the fabric from his injured back. He turned and faced the sun, letting it burn his face into leather. As much as his injuries on his back and across his chest bothered him, he reveled in the feel of the wind against his flesh and the sun warming him as he worked.

He took a long drink from the burlap water bag, stuffed the cork in the top, then went back to work. He used the pickax slowly, picking his target in the loose rock and making each stroke count. A dozen powerful strokes sent rock flying, then he switched to his shovel and mucked out the shallow hole he dug. Over and over he repeated the procedure until he had penetrated almost five feet into the hillside, reopening the Silver Jackass Mine.

He used his bandanna to mop his face, then hunkered down and pawed through the small chunks of rock he pulled from the mine shaft until he found the grainy black sand from the thicker vein now hidden under tons of fallen rock. Slocum pulled out Happy Harry's equipment and began working to do a rough-and-ready field assay of the rock. He could tell this was high-grade ore, but he had to be sure.

The alcohol-fed blowpipe burned brightly after he got it fired up using a lucifer from his shirt pocket and soon reduced the piece of ore to a tiny bead of silver in the charcoal crucible. Slocum rolled the shining molten bead about, then tapped it out. The bead fell into the sand and cooled instantly. Slocum fished it out, scraped sand off it, and looked at the pocked piece of silver.

He grinned when the bead easily yielded to pressure from his thumbnail. Happy Harry had been expert in doing the analysis and had warned Slocum about the chance of getting lead and mistaking it for silver. Slocum knew enough about silver, gold, and lead to recognize the real thing when he saw it.

"Silver," he said with some satisfaction. He needed a new assay done by an expert to be sure, but unless he missed by a country mile, the Silver Jackass would prove twice as profitable as they had originally thought. That means hundreds of thousands of dollars worth of silver waited to be plucked from the ground and turned into ingots, coins, and conchos.

He sucked in his breath as that thought fluttered across his brain.

"Missed the son of a bitch," he grumbled. "I need to practice my marksmanship. Too much time mining has ruined me." Slocum replayed the scene at the livery again. There was no reason in hell he ought to have missed the black-dressed shootist. But he had. There had not even been a feel of hitting the man before he hightailed it.

"And who were you talking to? Wish there had been time to track you both down."

"What's that, John?"

Slocum swung about, startled. He had been so lost in thought, first with the field assay and then his futile regret over missing the gunman when he had the chance, that he had grown careless. Anyone could have slugged him—or worse.

"Is your back bothering you?" Cara Penks came over and peered critically at him. "You should not expose such injuries to the sun. It can only cause problems healing."

"It's too hot to work with my shirt on. If anything, that makes my back hurt more."

"Perhaps so." She sounded like a nurse dissatisfied with her patient. "I brought some lunch. You have been working for hours and hours without a break. I thought you might like some company."

"Much obliged," Slocum said, wiping his face again. His bandanna came away wet and grimy. He knew what he must look like, but it didn't seem to bother Cara.

"I tried to clean up the shack, but there is no way to keep a dirt floor tidy," she said, sighing heavily. Slocum hoped this would be the only thing Cara Penks ever had to worry over again. They would bury her brother—or at least have a simple funeral service for him at the same time Happy Harry was buried—and then she could get on with her life.

"That's not important," Slocum said. "We won't be here that long."

"Why not? Aren't you finding any silver in this rock?" She kicked at a hunk of granite with a dainty foot.

"Not in *that* rock," Slocum said. "But in what's coming from the old mine, the rock is stuffed with silver. It almost leaps out. I could squeeze it and get droplets of silver."

Slocum thought Cara was going to ask to see him do that, then realized he was joking.

"The mine is rich, so why not work it right away?" she asked again.

"The deed. We need to make sure the land deed is properly registered and a copy is riding high in my pocket. Then we can decide what to do. It might be best to sell the mine to others. We could walk away with thousands of dollars."

"Thousands?" Cara bit her lip and looked into the shallow opening Slocum had carved back into the hillside. "Wouldn't we get even more by mining ourselves?"

"Over the years, we would. But this is hard work. Dangerous work," Slocum said, skirting around reminding her what had happened to her half brother. "I don't know if I'm cut out for the kind of work it would take, and I'm sure you're anxious to return home."

"Home," she said with a tinge of bitterness. "Where is that? Philadelphia? Hardly. My father is dead and there is no other family. I feel like your other partner, Mr. Harlan. He was alone, too, wasn't he?"

"Seems that way," Slocum allowed. "What about this Matthew you mentioned?" Slocum saw instant fire in the woman's eyes. Her mouth opened, then clamped shut, and she seemed to fold into herself. Cara wrapped her arms around her body and sat on the ground before drawing up her knees as if she might simply vanish.

"I didn't mean to pry into something that's none of my business," Slocum said. She looked up at him, so miserable he had to go to her and put his arm around her.

"He was an awful man," she said in a choked voice. "Not like you, John."

"You know nothing about me," Slocum said sharply. He had spent his life dodging the law and had killed more than one man. Some he had killed during the war simply because he had been ordered to. Others he had taken some delight in cutting down, and if he could find the bushwhacker who had shot him, he would add one more to that bloody list.

"I know all I need to know. You might be a violent man, but not with me." She snuggled closer and turned to him, her face close and her lips parted slightly. Slocum felt a mite uneasy, but her nearness and need were undeniable. He kissed her. Hard.

Cara surged over and on top of him, bearing him back to the ground. Slocum winced as the dirt cut into his back. Cara immediately saw his discomfort and rolled off, but her arms remained around him. Their faces just inches apart, she said in a soft voice, "Here, John. I want to make love here. Now."

"We're out in the open, in plain sight. What if someone sees us? Your reputation—"

"The devil take my reputation!" she flared. "What do I care for any of that? I want you *now!*"

She pulled him down powerfully, and there was no more chance to argue with her. Slocum felt her eager fingers working at his belt, pulling his jeans away. And somehow, as they wrestled passionately on the hard ground, he opened her blouse and exposed the twin mounds of her succulent, white-fleshed breasts. They shone like mounds of cream in the sunlight and he could not restrain himself.

He broke away from her mouth and moved down slowly, licking and kissing as he went. When he came to one breast, he slowly ran his tongue from the broad base all the way to the top where the nipple sat hard and pulsing amid a copper-colored disk. His tongue batted the lust-engorged nipple about, then left it quivering to go to the other.

"Oh, John, I'm on fire inside. Keep doing that. Don't stop, don't!" Cara pleaded. Her fingers ran over his sweat slickened arms and down his sides. He felt some pain as she brushed across the spot where he had been shot in the chest, but the pain wasn't enough to keep his body from responding to her ministrations.

Slocum felt himself hardening into an iron rod. He moved so he was between her slender legs and let her sit up enough to push his pants all the way down to his knees.

His erection quivered and bounced between them. He groaned softly when she circled it with her long fingers and began stroking gently.

Slocum blinked at the sight of her breasts so nakedly, so wantonly exposed, and wondered at her cultured veneer. It wasn't hard to get past her fine manners and release the animal lust locked within Cara Penks's trim, supple young body.

And Slocum wasn't even going to wonder at that. He slid his hands under her skirts and lifted the layers of cloth. His hands found the naked flesh of her legs and stroked along the smooth skin as he got the impeding cloth out of his way. The bright sunlight showed she wasn't wearing any of her frilly undergarments. He caught sight of the delightful gully all matted with midnight-black fur. His hand pressed down, and the response was immediate.

Cara stretched out full-length on the ground and writhed as her desires mounted.

"In, John, put it in."

"This?" he teased, his middle finger sliding along her lust-moistened nether lips and into her hot interior. He wiggled his finger back and forth until she was thrashing about on the ground like a fish out of water.

"No, don't, don't do that anymore. I want you. All of you!" She half sat up and grabbed at his quivering manhood, tugging him insistently toward her crotch. He slipped his finger from her and placed his hands over her breasts. He squeezed down hard and caught the nipples between thumbs and forefingers. Rolling the hard little buttons of flesh about sent her pulse racing; he felt it through the hillock of flesh he crushed under his palms. Her heart hammered away with the speed of a frightened fawn's.

And then he let her pull him directly to the spot they both desired most. The tip of his hardness brushed over the furred rim of her female fissure, then he was completely buried balls-deep in her.

For a moment neither of them moved. Slocum was paralyzed by the warmth and pressure surrounding him. He could only guess at the feelings coursing through Cara's trim body. And then she arched her back, lifted her buttocks off the ground and shoved herself up hard against him. Slocum's willpower vanished. He could not restrain himself—and there was no need.

Hard and fast he began stroking in and out of her. Her inner juices lubricated the wild, unsparing movement and

allowed their passions to build to the breaking point. Slocum's balls hardened, tightened, came to a boil. Just before
he spilled his seed into her wanton cavity, Cara let out a
shriek of glee and shook all over like a quaking aspen in a
high wind. She clutched at him and pulled him down so he
could never escape—as if he wanted to.

He rammed forward and exploded within her. This
movement caused a second tremor to pass through Cara,
lifting her again off the ground. She drove herself into him
as fervently as he drove forward. And then they both sank
to the ground, sweating and exhausted from their efforts.

"It was never like this before I met you, John," she said
in a low voice.

"You're quite an inspiring sight," he told her. "Sometimes, it gets to be a chore to keep my hands off you when
we're in public." Slocum pushed away slightly and tried
to look around. They were miles from Virginia City and
not many had reason to come down the road to the Silver
Jackass Mine. Still, they were out under the broad blue sky
and anyone could see them from miles and miles away, if
they were up on the mountain slopes.

"Don't worry so, John. My reputation does not matter."

"It does," he contradicted. "A lady's reputation is like
a man's—it's about all we can really claim as our own. If
a man gets known as a liar or a back-shooter, that will dog
him to the grave. If a woman is known to have loose
morals, well, every woman will scorn her and every man
will—". He bit off his words.

"Every man will want her to prove her loose morals?"
Cara teased. "I have no desire to share myself with any
other man. You are quite enough for me, thank you, Mr.
Slocum."

"I appreciate the confidence you have in me," Slocum
said, sitting up. He forced himself to look away from her
nakedness. She still lay with her slender legs lifted and bent
at the knees. And her luscious white breasts quivered
slightly as she moved, tempting treats for any man and

possibly more than Slocum deserved.

"Shall we eat the lunch I brought?" Cara Penks sat up and arranged her clothing. Slocum watched her, feeling stirrings once more in his loins. But she was right. This dalliance was an unexpected bonus for the work he had done that morning. More work lay ahead of him, and making love to the beautiful woman again wouldn't get any of it done, no matter how satisfying that might be to Slocum.

They ate in silence for a while, then Cara said, "I'm not a very good cook, am I?"

Slocum shrugged. "Beats eating my own cooking. I barely survived more than one trail."

"Why don't I believe you?" She laughed and cleaned up the remains from their meal and tucked it back into the basket she had carried from the shack. "I'll let you get back to work."

"A few more hours working on the mine ought to get me all I need to prove this claim, even to a Carson City bureaucrat," Slocum said, eyeing the faint outline of the original mine opening. He watched Cara go back down the hill, her aching beauty giving him reason to work all the harder the rest of the day. Before sundown, he had accumulated almost an ounce of silver from the field assaying and more than ten pounds of nuggets and black sand that would turn heads and bring buyers running when he flashed them around.

After dinner, Slocum and Cara sat outside the cabin and watched the stars come and go behind veils of high clouds. He was aware of her nearness, yet a new gulf had grown between them.

"Tomorrow," she said after a long silence, "we go to Carson City?"

"Reckon so. I have what I need from the Silver Jackass. It shouldn't take more than two days to get to the south and west, another day to establish the claim all over."

"And then, John? What then?"

"Harry needs burying and there's the matter of a service for your brother."

"I've made arrangements with the undertaker," she said. "He told me you wouldn't mind a double ceremony. I approved it. But that's not really what I meant. What of all . . . this?" Her hand moved in a wide arc, taking in all the countryside. But Slocum knew what she meant.

"We determine a fair value for the mine. I find a buyer, and then I'll pay you half."

"It seems so unfair, women not being allowed to own property," she said.

"Wyoming's agitating to give women the vote," Slocum said. "Won't be long before other states follow suit. Who knows where that will end? Why not women being allowed to own land?"

She moved closer and they sat, staring into the distance, saying nothing. Slocum knew what really went through her mind, and he couldn't answer the unspoken questions. What would they do after the Silver Jackass was sold and accounts settled? They'd both be a danged sight richer than they were now, but would she want to return to Philadelphia? Or would she make a fuss about staying with him?

Slocum couldn't sort out what he felt for her—and what it meant to him to be able to climb onto a horse, find a bright star in the dark night sky, and simply ride toward it without considering anyone else. Settling down came to him in dreams sometimes, but he was never sure if he could handle it. He had grown up on a farm and knew the work well. He had made crops grow that neither his father nor his brother Robert could, but that had been before the war.

Slocum wasn't sure if he was running from ghosts or toward a future he only vaguely glimpsed. Cara might play a part in that future, but he simply couldn't say. Not now, not yet.

He pushed to his feet suddenly when he heard something from the direction of the mine.

"What's wrong, John?"

"Maybe nothing. Thought I heard somebody prowling around." He reached inside the door of the mining shack and grabbed his six-shooter. Strapping it on, he started for the Silver Jackass.

"John, don't. You can't go out there. You might get hurt! Shot again!"

"If it's who I think, confronting him is better than letting him murder us in our sleep," Slocum said grimly. "Go on into the cabin and lock the door. It's not much, but it ought to keep you safe."

"You mean someone might try to harm me?" The fear rose in Cara's voice.

"Not likely. I won't be gone long." He kissed her quickly and guided her toward the open door to the cabin. He hadn't done much to fix up the ramshackle building. And barring the door wouldn't do more than slow down a man intent on harming Cara, but it might give her a sense of safety.

"Please be careful," she urged. Her hand rested on his arm, then slipped away as she vanished into the black maw of the mining shack. Slocum waited for her to wrestle shut the door and bar it. Then he checked his Colt Navy, made sure all six chambers were charged, then started for the mine.

He reached the Silver Jackass just as the moon poked above the mountaintops, but the silvery light did nothing to show him where the prowler hid. Slocum circled the area where he had spent the day working, hunting for any trace of the intruder. He found a glowing cigarette butt on the ground and crushed it with his bootheel.

Slocum hadn't smoked a cigarette since coming to Virginia City, never getting around to buying the fixings in town. Testing the air with his keen nose, he found the thin trail of smoke leading up the hillside. Proceeding cautiously, he let the half moon rise farther to give him as much light as possible for the trek.

Slocum knew the terrain well and made good time, but

he became anxious about the moonlight. If he could see by it, so could the prowler. As he made his way up the hill, he slowly realized he was heading straight for the spot where he had seen Arly Penks talking with the gunman.

He came to the level spot and looked around. He saw nothing, but his sensitive nose told him someone was nearby. Slocum's hand flashed toward his six-gun as strong hands shoved against his shoulders. He groped for purchase and found none.

He hit the ground hard enough to knock the wind from his lungs and started rolling down the mountainside.

13

Over and over Slocum rolled, wincing as the prickly pear pads stabbed at him, moaning as sharp rock cut at his back and chest, unable to stop other spiny vegetation from tearing at his exposed face. Slocum tried to keep his eyes shut but could not help but notice the dim flashing as he rolled faceup to the moon and then facedown. But always he went down the steep hillside with bone-jarring force until he crashed into a scrub oak and swung about, bent double around the trunk.

Shaken, not fully conscious, Slocum got to his feet and immediately toppled backward to lie in a sandy arroyo. Again the wind gusted from his tortured lungs. The faint lights he saw through his eyelids vanished when he passed out.

How long he lay knocked out from the fall Slocum couldn't say. The sound of boots crunching heavily against the stone on the mountainside brought him around with a start. His hand weakly reached for his Colt Navy and found nothing. His six-shooter had come out of the cross-draw holster during his precipitous fall. Biting his lip to keep from crying out and betraying his position to his pursuer,

Slocum got to his hands and knees and tried to clear his vision. Several seconds passed before he focused on the rocky slope above him.

He clenched his hands into fists, ready for a fight to the death against his unseen assailant. No one tossed him down a mountain, then came hunting with the intent to kill him. Without his six-gun the fight might be one-sided, but Slocum would let the son of a bitch know he had faced a real opponent before dying.

"Where'd he go? I can't find him anywhere," came the whiny voice of the gunman.

Mumbled commands came from above, probably from the spot where Slocum had started his fall. He tried to make out the words but failed. Try as he might, he couldn't even identify whether the voice was male or female or if more than one person spoke. He needed to know how many men he faced. If he could get to the shootist, a sudden rush might bowl him over long enough to grab his six-shooter.

A six-gun resting in his hand went a long way toward evening the odds.

"He's dead, I tell you," the gunman said from only a few yards away. "Nobody could survive a tumble like that. There's blood to hell and gone." Slocum caught the reflection of moonlight against silver conchos. The gunslinger might as well have lit a signal fire; those ornaments betrayed him completely with every step he took. Slocum moved slowly, weaving drunkenly from the dull pain throughout his body. The places that weren't torn up were pierced by cactus thorns.

The scrub oak that had halted his uncontrollable fall downhill rustled slightly. Slocum bent down and picked up a rock, ready to crown the gunman when he showed himself. For almost a minute, Slocum waited, but the shootist didn't appear. Worried that he might have been circled, Slocum glanced over his shoulder and studied the shadowy terrain of the arroyo. He saw no movement.

When a wind kicked up, Slocum knew he wouldn't be

able to hear the gunslinger's movements as easily. Whistling sounds from the wind in the low trees masked the sound of the gunfighter moving in the dark. Slocum struck out on his own, cutting down the bone-dry arroyo until he found another scrub oak on the high verge and pulled himself up. Over the gully rim, he lay on his belly and watched for movement. Nothing but the restless shifting of the low vegetation from the cold night wind revealed itself.

Slocum cursed. He had the feeling the gunman was close, but he couldn't spot him. Clutching the sharp rock he had found, Slocum inched forward, occasionally halting to search for the shootist.

Slocum's belly tightened into a knot when he spotted the dim outline of a man in front of him, not ten yards distant. Slocum rubbed his eyes to clear some of the blurring, then got to his feet and advanced cautiously. The wind hid the sounds of his clumsy approach now. Slocum knew he would have been dead if he had tried closing on an Indian, but the gunfighter was oblivious to the world around him.

With only a few feet between them, Slocum launched himself. The rock rose in a high arc that ended on the top of the man's skull. The impact sent a shock of pain rippling down Slocum's arm and caused him to recoil. His heel caught on a rock, and he sat down heavily.

But the gunman hadn't stirred. Slocum shook his head again and his vision cleared enough for him to see that he had attacked an overhanging tree limb. Frightened for a split second that he might have drawn unwanted attention to himself by the futile attack, Slocum scrambled to his feet. Then he realized he was alone.

Angry with himself for failing to find the gunman, Slocum ranged farther afield, moving in a crisscrossing pattern to the point where he had smashed into the scrub oak. Looking uphill, he saw no trace of the shootist or his partner. Cursing under his breath, Slocum dropped to one knee and located the path he had taken tumbling down the hill. Working up the mountainside, Slocum finally found the spot where his Colt had caught in the tangle of a low-growing vine.

"Now, let's get down to it," Slocum said softly. Six-shooter in hand and ready for action, he climbed the precipitous hill with long strides that eventually brought him to the flat area. But it took only a few minutes to convince Slocum he was alone on the mountain. He found tracks going down the far side of the hill, toward the mining shack where he had left Cara.

"I'll shoot your black hearts out if you've harmed her!" he raged. Throwing caution to the winds, Slocum bulled his way down the faint path he had taken to the top. He ran to within a few yards of the cabin before he hesitated.

Growing careful again, Slocum circled the cabin, hunting for spoor. He found two sets of footprints going in. Whether any came out he could not tell. There were too many rocky patches that would mask any trace of departure. Crouched low, Slocum moved closer.

His vision blurred again, then sharpened. Slocum made out the outline of a man standing in the doorway. With a motion born of long practice, the six-shooter came up and centered perfectly. The single shot Slocum got off sent splinters flying through the air. He ran forward, intent on keeping the gunman's partner from harming Cara, if he held her prisoner.

Slocum took a deep breath and let it out slowly when he saw how his eyes had deceived him again. He had sent a slug through the door. The cabin was as empty as a whore's promise.

"Damnation," Slocum said, rubbing his head. His body hurt like all the demons of hell had poked him with pitchforks, and his vision kept wavering. "Must have hit my head harder than I thought."

A large lump, tender to the touch, formed just above his left eye. Slocum cursed some more as he left the cabin and saw that his jackass was gone, along with the sturdy wagon that had served him and his partners so well. He walked a dozen paces in the direction taken by the wagon, then grew so dizzy he stumbled.

Realizing he was at the end of his rope, Slocum returned to the shack and fell full length on his blanket. Sharp pain assailed him, and he knew he could never sleep with so many cactus spines in his hide. Sitting up, Slocum worked until he grew so weak he could hardly hold his knife. When he collapsed this time, he didn't even notice the pain from his injuries.

Slocum sneezed and came awake just after sunrise. He felt a little better but not much. He had to rely on stark anger to drive him. Using water in a bucket, he washed the grime off himself. He patched himself up the best he could, then ate from the provender he had laid up for the trip to Carson City. His belly full and his hide repaired the best he could, Slocum looked to the path taken by the kidnapping gunman and Cara Penks.

In the bright light of day, Slocum had no trouble finding the wagon tracks. Settling his six-shooter at his side and throwing a burlap bag of food over his shoulder, he started walking. Slocum knew that the jackass wouldn't pull well for another driver, and he had the gunman pegged as an impatient man.

But why kidnap Cara Penks? That made no sense to him. The coldness in Slocum's gut returned when he thought of the one reason the gunman might have. It had nothing to do with claim jumping or ransom. It had everything to do with defiling the woman.

Slocum's stride lengthened as he turned south on the road, following the wagon. He reckoned the gunfighter had six or eight hours start on him. With a balky mule and a struggling prisoner, the kidnapper might not have put too many miles behind him. The only good thing Slocum could see in this was that the wagon was heading toward Carson City.

A short break for a noon meal refreshed Slocum and gave spring to his walk again. Just before sundown he heard the braying of the jackass from around the bend in the road. Slocum studied the terrain, then cut off the road and took to the sloping hill ahead of him. He got to the top and peered down at the winding road. A smile crossed his lips. Below him stood the wagon and the jackass, still braying and complaining loudly, but there was no one nearby to hear the noisy protests.

Slocum saw a small stand of trees and a stream meandering from higher in the mountains. He guessed this might be where the gunman had taken Cara.

Slipping and sliding, ignoring a score of new scrapes, Slocum made his way down the hillside as fast as he could. He approached the jackass and soothed the donkey, then slipped his six-gun from his holster and went hunting.

"Don't touch me, you monster!" came Cara's loud cry of resistance to the gunman's overtures. Slocum's heart told him to hurry; his head told him to bide his time. Rushing now might mean a mistake that would leave Slocum dead and Cara Penks doomed.

He entered the small grove and used the pine trees for cover as he neared the stream. Slocum fought to keep his hand from lifting his six-gun and getting off a quick shot, but he held back. The shootist had Cara staked out spread-eagle on the ground beside the stream. He knelt beside her, not giving Slocum the clean shot he needed. If he missed, he might hit the bound woman.

"You'll love every minute of this," the gunman promised her. "And why not? I'm just about the best there is, on either side of the Mississippi."

"Go to hell!" raged Cara.

"Such language. Or is that the way you fillies from Philadelphia like it? You want me to treat you like a two-bit whore?" The man tossed his concho-studded hat aside and reached down to unfasten his belt.

Slocum stepped out. Cara's eyes widened. Her mouth opened and closed like a fish out of water. Then she regained her wits and cried, "Kill him, John. Shoot him down like the snake he is!"

"Now, little lady, that kinda of trick don't work with me. I thought you were smarter than that."

"John, do it. Don't give him a chance. He's trying to . . . to have his way with me!" Cara thrashed about, pulling hard at the ropes holding her to the ground. One breast came free from her blouse and flopped about nakedly as she struggled.

"Now that's about as delectable a sight as I ever have seen. What else are you hidin' from me?"

"She's not hiding anything," Slocum said coldly. "I ought to take her advice and bushwhack you. But that would make you and me the same. We're not."

"What?" The gunman leaped to his feet and swung around to face Slocum. "You died back there. I know it. So much blood."

"I've got enough left in my veins to take care of a buzzard like you," Slocum said. His stance widened and his mind settled into a calm that always came upon him before a fight. Every sense heightened, and he saw and heard and smelled things he never did otherwise.

He smelled the fear in the black-clad shootist. The gunman's hand trembled and sweat popped out on his forehead. He saw the flaring of the man's nostrils and the throbbing of a vein on the side of the man's neck. Slocum could almost hear the harsh breathing.

"You're gonna die, Slocum. You humiliated me back there in the saloon. Nobody throws my six-shooters into a stove. You ruined two perfectly good guns."

"You tried to dry-gulch me twice," Slocum said, not wanting to argue the man to death. He knew all the gun-fighting tricks and had used most of them himself. Trying to distract him from the job at hand wasn't possible. "There won't be a third time."

Slocum's hand moved faster than chain lighting. He cleared leather, whipped the gun around, and fanned the hammer to get off the first shot. A second wasn't needed.

The gunman's hands closed inches above the butts of the six-shooters shoved into his belt. His eyes went wider and an expression of stark surprise crossed his face. Death left it there. The man's knees buckled, and he sank into a boneless pile.

"John!"

Slocum's attention shifted from the corpse to the wooded area around him. He knew there had been a second man on the mountain. Where was he now?

"Are you all right?" Cara seemed more worried about him than he had been about her.

"The other one. Where is he?"

"What other one? He was alone. I never saw anyone else. He came in and slugged me. When I came to, I was trussed up and couldn't do anything after he tossed me into the wagon. Oh, John, John!"

Slocum didn't go straightaway to free her. He stopped beside the fallen gunman and rolled the man over with his boot. Slocum stared at the face, now pale in death, and wondered who the hell he was and why he had it in for a man he had never met before that night in the Virginia City saloon.

14

"John, get me free!" protested Cara Penks. "Don't just stand there."

Slocum didn't answer the bound woman right away. He kicked the gunman's ribs again as hard as he could and got no response. Seldom could a man fake death so completely without showing some faint sign of life. To be certain, Slocum sank to one knee and pressed his hand against the unmoving chest. No heartbeat. Slocum's hand came away bloody from the gunfighter's chest. Slocum had drilled the shootist squarely through the heart.

"All right," Slocum said. "The danger's past." He reached over and fumbled at Cara's bonds. In a few seconds, the woman was free and as angry as a wet hen.

"How dare he!" she raged.

"He won't be doing much of anything to harm you now," Slocum observed. "You recognize him?"

This caused Cara to stop her tirade for a moment. She stared at the gunman's pale, pinched face as if for the first time. One hand went to her mouth as she shook her head.

"I don't recognize him. He's dead. You killed him, John."

"He would have done worse to you," Slocum pointed out. "I don't know who he is, either." Slocum fumbled in the man's shirt pocket and pulled out a wad of greenbacks thick enough to choke a cow. Blood had stained the money, but this didn't bother Slocum too much. He deserved anything the dead man might give up as payment for all he had been through. He tucked the bills into his own shirt pocket.

"Mighty fine silver work," Slocum said, running his finger over the conchos on the gunman's hat. He found one concho missing on the side of the left leg, then frowned when he studied those on the right thigh. One had been scratched repeatedly, gouges dug into the soft silver.

"What caused that?" Slocum wondered aloud.

"It looks as if he struck friction matches on the metal," Cara said, peering over Slocum's shoulder. She still appeared shaken at being so close to a dead man—or her own death—but bravely fought to overcome her shock.

"You may be right," Slocum said. He imagined the gunman reaching into a pocket, pulling out a lucifer, and dragging it across the concho to ignite it. The decoration was at the precise point where it would be easiest to strike. And then what did the man do?

"He would toss the lucifer into a pile of papers soaked with kerosene." Slocum answered his own unspoken question. "He's the one who killed Happy Harry and maybe set the fire in Gold Hill that burned everyone there out of house and home."

Slocum scratched his head as he tried to figure out what the gunman got from the arson. He might have covered his murder of Harry Harlan with the fire, but the fire captain had said the registrar's office had been a special target for the firebug. And the fire in Gold Hill had been strikingly similar. One thing Slocum had learned about professional killers was their predictability. Once they found a successful pattern, they stuck with it through thick and thin.

There wasn't any reason Slocum could see that an arsonist wouldn't be the same way.

"I think he might have killed Happy Harry, then set fire to the doctor's office to hide it," Slocum said. "He's a low-down, no-account snake in the grass. He's better off dead." He didn't have to convince himself. He spoke only for Cara to understand that the killing had been necessary.

"This wasn't the first time he had done something like . . . like he was going to do to me, was it?" she asked, a stammer in her voice. "He would have had his way with me, murdered me or left me to die staked out here, and then done it all over with some other poor woman."

"Reckon so," Slocum said. He stumbled a little as he found Cara suddenly in his arms. Her tears burst forth like a summer thunderstorm and soaked hotly into his shirt. He held her until the quaking of her body stopped. She pushed back and dabbed at her eyes. The tears left grimy tracks down her cheeks.

"I am being so foolish. I don't know what possessed me to act like that," she said almost primly.

"You never saw him before he kidnapped you?" Slocum kicked at the corpse again. He was considering not bothering with a burial. The back-shooting son of a bitch didn't deserve it, and digging a grave was harder work than he wanted to do right now.

Cara shook her head. Her dark hair flew in wild disarray, strands glued together with dirt and sweat.

"He was paid well for what he did," Slocum said, touching the greenbacks in his pocket. He tried to figure who might be willing to hire a gunman and couldn't. Shrugging it off, he began stripping anything of value from the body.

"What are you doing, John? Robbing the dead?" This shocked Cara as much as the notion the man was going to rape her.

"Getting him ready for burial," Slocum said, her concern forcing him into digging a grave. "Unless you want to leave him out for the buzzards and coyotes." The shudder that shook her body told him her answer. "You go on down to the stream and clean up. I'll tend to this chore."

Cara nodded and rushed off, thankful for this respite from a distasteful responsibility. Slocum spun the cylinders in the man's two six-shooters, critically eyed the triggers and barrels, and figured he could get five dollars apiece for the pistols. The conchos might melt into a nugget of silver worth ten or twenty dollars. He plucked the round decorations from hat and pants, studying the one used to strike the lucifers more closely.

Slocum sniffed and detected the pungent phosphorus odor distinctive to lucifers. That convinced him he was right. The man had set the fires in Virginia City. Nowhere on the body did Slocum find fixings for a smoke or even a plug chewing tobacco. The gunman didn't use tobacco, as far as Slocum could tell from the man's fingers and their lack of discoloration from cigarettes.

The memory of good tobacco smoke rolling down his throat and into his lungs turned him wistful. He would see to getting a pack of papers and a pouch of tobacco once he got to Carson City. It had been too long since he had indulged in a good smoke.

Slocum dragged the body to one side of the small meadow where the gunman had intended to do his worst with Cara. Slocum poked around in the back of the wagon and found a shovel. It took him almost a half hour to dig a hole deep enough to keep the body safe from coyotes. Slocum rolled the corpse into the hole, left the gunman lying facedown, and started shoveling dirt back in.

When a mound remained, Slocum brushed off his hands and wiped at sweat on his forehead. "It was better than you deserved," Slocum said with a touch of malice. As he had dug, he had begun to feel cheated. The man had died much too fast to suit him.

And he had not given up the information Slocum needed most. Who had hired the black-clad stranger and to what end were the fires set? Hundreds of people might have died from either fire.

"I feel much refreshed," Cara said, coming up. Her clothing clung to her wet body. Slocum admired the sleek figure for a moment, then replied.

"I can use a scrubbing, myself. I've been through hell and walked back barefoot." He shrugged out of his shirt, revealing the new cuts and scrapes.

Cara gasped. "You look like a pincushion. You have thorns everywhere!" She tentatively reached out and rubbed her finger over one stubby end. Slocum jerked away. The pain from the cactus spines he had missed hadn't bothered him until she touched the one.

"Get a needle and pry a few more out. I did the best I could, and I reckon it wasn't too good."

Cara drew a pin from her skirts and began working on him. He winced but said nothing, his thoughts distant. When Cara had finished, he still had not come up with a good idea of the puzzle facing them. The gunman hadn't acted like the usual scum that drifted from one town to another looking for a fast buck and a loose woman.

"I'll scrub you down, John," Cara said. Slocum looked into her bright eyes and smiled.

"That's about the finest thing that's been said to me in quite a while. I accept your offer."

An hour later, clean and feeling chipper enough to fight his weight in wildcats, Slocum and Cara got into the wagon and headed it along the road toward Carson City.

Slocum had to keep snapping the reins against the jackass' rump to make him move. Once they had reached the outskirts of Carson City, the animal had begun balking because of the heavier traffic on the roads. Wagons groaning under the weight of supplies raced into the city and treasure coaches laden with silver left. Men on horses trotted on all sides and the addition of children playing and women on their way to market made the donkey downright stubborn.

"Oh, John," Cara said, trying to brush her dark hair from her eyes. "We cannot be seen like this."

"There's nothing wrong with a man and woman travel-ing together," Slocum said, his mind already focused on the buildings ahead. He saw the capitol building ahead and knew the state repository for land deeds had to be nearby. The closer he had gotten to Carson City, the more he yearned for the piece of paper in his pocket proving he was the rightful owner of the Silver Jackass Mine. Not knowing who paid the gunman to work his corrupt ways chewed at Slocum like a hungry rat.

Until he knew his true enemies, he would never rest easy. Worse, Cara Penks might be in jeopardy, too.

"Nobody knows us here," he said, distracted by the nearness of two men galloping their horses past, racing for some unknown prize. "We'll be safe."

"No, John, I mean the way we *look*. We are a positive fright, like something the cat dragged in. I cannot be seen looking so . . . so disheveled."

Slocum had to laugh. After all they had been through, appearances didn't mean spit to him. They were alive and respectably enough clothed and that was all that mattered to him.

"Look at some of the miners going into the city," Slo-cum said. "They're worse off than we are—than we ever could be." The hard-rock miners and prospectors who had come to the capital to file their claims stretched in an end-less river, or so it seemed to him. Slocum found himself eyeing the men suspiciously, wondering if one of them might be the claim jumper out to bamboozle him out of the Silver Jackass.

Such thinking got him nowhere, he realized. If he started shooting at shadows, he would find himself in a stewpot of trouble. Carson City had more deputies patrolling than about any city he could remember. The huge flow of silver from the Comstock Lode drew thieves, as well as those of incredible prosperity. He had heard it said there were al-most as many lawmen in Carson City as whorehouses.

From the glint of sunlight off badges, he believed it might be true.

He snapped the reins against the jackass again and got the balky donkey moving. Slocum had to use every bit of his skill driving the wagon when they passed through the crowded market and maneuvered the wagon into a narrow alley running parallel to the main street.

"Hey, mister," Slocum called. "There a livery where I can get my donkey fed?"

An indolent man lounging in front of a small store lifted his gaze, studied Slocum like a wolf sizing up a lamb, then grunted and pointed down the street. "Turn left, two blocks. Go straight. Follow the smell. You cain't miss ol' man O'Connor's stable. He's got barrels in front of it to mark his territory."

"Much obliged," Slocum said, heading in the direction of the stables. He shook his head in wonder when he saw the barrels the drifter had mentioned. The stable owner had painted them bright orange. Slocum dismounted and led the jackass through the maze formed in front of the wide livery doors.

"Need to leave my rig here for a spell," he said to a blond, ruddy-faced man coming from the stable.

"You come to the right place. Ol' Danny O'Connor offers the best service in the whole danged capital. Two dollars silver, five if you pay in scrip, and the beast's sides will be a-bulgin' from the feed."

Slocum peeled off five bills from the roll taken off the dead gunman. He passed them over. The stable owner's eyes widened when he saw the blood on the greenbacks, but he said nothing.

"The lady and I need to get to the land office. Where might I find it?"

"You passed by it on the way in. Smallish building, two-story brick front. Next to the Wells Fargo office. You can't miss that. Looks like every other Wells Fargo office in the world."

Slocum touched the brim of his Stetson in acknowledgment, took Cara's arm, and led her away from the stable. The jackass brayed and started kicking when O'Connor unhitched it. Slocum knew the man had his hands full, but that mattered less than getting to the registrar of deeds and getting a copy of the Silver Jackass title.

"I wish we could linger, John. This is such a cosmopolitan town compared to Virginia City."

"More people, maybe more money, but I doubt it," he said, looking around for the Wells Fargo office. He had never been in a town where the company deviated from their basic design: a brick building with iron shutters and their sign. He spotted it halfway down the street.

"Really?" Cara seemed surprised at this. "Look how well the people dress."

"They're picking up the crumbs from the feast," Slocum said. "Big money in the rock around Mount Davidson and down Gold Canyon. The Comstock is about the richest silver lode ever found, bar none. The men working those claims might not dress too opulently, but there are more millionaires in Virginia City than here."

"Possibly so. I had the privilege of looking around Gold Hill before it burned," Cara said. "The homes there were quite spacious and richly appointed. I especially liked the iron fences and the lacy wood gingerbread decoration on the gables."

"Eilly Orrum and Sandy Bowers made more millions than either of us will ever see, and they're living in Gold Hill—or were," Slocum said, wondering if the earliest of miners in Virginia City had lost their houses and belongings in the gunman's fire.

He walked past the Wells Fargo office and stopped in front of the building with gilt letters neatly stenciled on the window. Through these doors passed all the land deeds and claims to riches in the entire territory. Slocum felt his heart beating a mite faster at the thought of being rich—and how he might have to go to great lengths to prove himself worthy of the silver.

"I will vouch for you, John. Do not worry over that point," Cara said in her prim, schoolmarm fashion. Slocum had to laugh.

"I'm looking for a copy of the deed, nothing more. When I have it tucked away, then I'll see to getting Happy Harry's and your brother's portion."

Slocum opened the door for Cara and followed her into the cool, dim interior. A half dozen clerks toiled at desks behind the long, stained wooden counter. Slocum tried to guess how many sweaty arms had rested on this counter as deeds were filed. He couldn't count that high.

"Help you?" A portly man sporting only a thin halo of hair around his bald head pushed himself out of a protesting desk chair. As he came to the counter, he pushed up a visor onto his forehead and rubbed his ink-stained hands together. Black cuff protectors kept his work from blotting onto his shirt cuffs.

"You looking to record a deed?"

"I need a duplicate," Slocum said. "Mine got destroyed while fighting a fire in Virginia City." He took out the yellow foolscap deed and laid it on the counter. Parts broke off when the clerk pushed at it with his finger. He smirked and stared straight at Slocum.

"No way in hell—excuse my language, ma'am—this means anything. Had you filed with the Virginia City recorder?"

"I had. His records were destroyed in the fire. That's why he told me to get a copy."

"Good advice. What's the name on the claim?"

Slocum gave all three names. The sharp look he received from the clerk turned him wary.

"No fooling," the clerk said. "I've got the record book right here." He reached under the counter and hefted a huge ledger. Dropping it with a bang onto the counter, he stepped back and stared at Slocum.

"Why do you have it so readily available?" asked Cara. "That seems a bit of a coincidence."

"That's not the only coincidence, ma'am," the clerk said coldly. He ran his finger down the side, found a tab, and flipped the huge book open. A quick stab pointed out an entry still smudged and wet.

"You started to change the registry on the mine," Cara said. "You stopped. I don't understand."

"I always think it suspicious when considerable activity surrounds one piece of land. Seems a gent came in here yesterday with documents showing him to be the sole owner of the mine. His partners had signed over the property to him, or so he said."

"You changed the registration?" asked Slocum.

"Nope. Those quit claims he carried looked to be forgeries to me. Bad ones. But I told him I'd contact the Virginia City registrar and see what I could find out. He hightailed it out of here like he had his nose in a wringer."

"You have the quit claims handy?" Slocum asked. "I'd like to see them."

"Here they be." The clerk pulled them out of an envelope fastened to the page in the ledger. He shoved them across to Slocum.

There wasn't much reason for Slocum to go over the detailed and fraudulent pages since he already knew whose signature as new owner of the Silver Jackass would reside at the bottom.

Arly Penks had not been clever enough in his forgery scheme to steal the Silver Jackass Mine.

15

"My brother?" Cara Penks stared at the smudged ink entry in amazement. "But he's dead!"

"Excuse me, ma'am," said the portly clerk. He scratched his clean-shaven chin and adjusted his visor. "You telling me Arlin Penks is your brother?"

"Half brother," Slocum supplied. "She had been thinking Arly Penks died in a mine explosion. You can verify that with Doc Hanley down in Virginia City—and the undertaker."

"Arthur?" The clerk speared Slocum with his gaze.

"That's the funeral parlor owner's name," Slocum said, thinking back on his talk with the undertaker, trying to remember all he could of the unpleasant man. "Arthur Conroy. Or you can even telegraph Sheriff Tyler. He's had more than his share of dead in town lately, but he will remember the situation."

"Good to have names. You're Slocum, and this is one of your partners' sister." He coughed slightly. "Half sister," he corrected himself before Cara could say anything. "I didn't buy the forgeries." He tapped a pudgy finger on the quit claims. "But you have the ring of truth in what

141

you say. So, Mr. Slocum, let me contact the responsible parties down in Virginia City and verify your story. That's no problem, is it?''

"Here," Slocum said, pulling out twenty dollars in greenbacks. "This ought to cover the cost of the telegrams and your trouble in the matter."

The clerk snorted in disgust. "Your Mr. Penks, if that was even his name, offered me a hundred. I didn't take it."

"Sir," Cara said in her prim, Philadelphia manner, "this is *not* a bribe. It is to cover your expenses contacting the people most likely to provide the truth. I thought to bury my brother alongside Mr. Slocum's other partner, Mr. Harlan. Verify it all with Mr. Conroy."

"I've known Arthur half my life," the clerk mused. "He is an odd character but—"

"You knew him in Sacramento?" Slocum said, taking a shot in the dark.

"Why, yes. I reckon you do know him."

"He knew Happy Harry Harlan, too." Slocum saw the cloud of doubt vanish in the clerk's eyes. Pushing any more would accomplish nothing. If the clerk got the telegrams off and any of the men responded, Slocum was assured of his full title to the Silver Jackass.

"When will you—" started Cara, still intent on pushing the clerk. Slocum had dealt with land office clerks before and knew they could do no better than what they had already accomplished. He grabbed her elbow and steered her toward the door.

"We'll return in a couple hours," Slocum said, drowning out Cara's protests.

The clerk nodded, rubbing his fingers over the money Slocum had left on the counter. From the way he furtively glanced around, Slocum guessed none of it would find its way into official coffers. This petty theft didn't matter to Slocum if it won him his deed.

"He should have given us some firm commitment to pursue this to the utmost, John," said Cara, struggling in his grip. Slocum didn't relent and neither did she. "We can go back in there and let him know we will tolerate no dalliance!"

"Don't get so hot under the collar. He'll send the telegrams. I saw it in his face. He may not be the most honest man in Carson City, but he will do his job."

Cara Penks simmered down and walked along on Slocum's arm for several minutes before speaking.

"Is he dead or not?"

Slocum knew she meant her half brother. He, too, had been worrying at that like a dog with a bone. Not finding any trace of Penks's body ought to have told him something was bad wrong, but events had moved too fast—and Happy Harry had been badly injured in the same blast.

Memory of how he had cut up his back turned Slocum cold inside. The premature explosion might have been intended to kill two partners in the Silver Jackass Mine: Harry Harlan and John Slocum. And it might have been set by Arly Penks. That fit together better than anything else he could think up.

"I can't say, but we should try to find who is coming to town with forged documents." As they walked, Slocum's mind raced, turning over what he could do. He remembered Penks on the hillside above the mine, and he again recalled seeing the flash of silver. Hand moving to his jeans pocket, he ran a finger over the outline of the conchos taken from the dead gunman. Things pieced together, but Slocum still had to guess about too much. He didn't even know for a fact that Arly Penks still lived.

"What can you tell me about your brother?" Slocum asked.

"Very little, actually. I remember him, but I am not even sure I could recognize him if he came down the street toward us." Cara fumbled in her reticule and pulled out a photograph. "This is one my father had taken before Arlin left home."

Slocum glanced at the picture. He didn't put much store

in such things, never understanding why people sat in the painful braces for long minutes for a piece of paper. Some Indians thought the cameras stole their souls. Slocum wouldn't argue too much with them on the point.

"Might be Arly," Slocum allowed. "He's changed, and not for the best. Harder, less hair."

"A scar," Cara said suddenly. "Arlin had a long scar on his left leg just below the knee. About this long." She held out her hands and moved her fingers about ten inches apart.

"Can't say I ever saw a scar, or if I did, that it made any impression," Slocum said. "What are your half brother's preferences in food? Drink? Women?"

"Women? I can hardly say on that score, John." She averted her bright blue eyes and blushed. Slocum continued to be surprised at her reactions. He had to remind himself constantly that she was unused to the West, and life in Philadelphia was far different.

"He had a fondness for redheads," Slocum said, harkening back to the times he and his partners had gone into Virginia City to blow off steam. "And big steaks. He could eat like no man I ever saw. I swear, he must have had a hollow leg."

"Arlin did have an appetite," Cara said, finding refuge in this safe topic. "He often ate everything in the pantry, causing friction with Father."

"Carson City must have a hundred restaurants. There must be a man who came in and ate more than his size could account for. You go around and show this picture. It might nudge someone's memory."

"What about you, John?"

Slocum patted his shirt pocket. He still had a goodly amount of the money taken from the fallen shootist.

"I can get by," Slocum said, knowing some would be spent on bribes for information that would prove wrong. "Meet me back in front of the land office at four o'clock."

"John, will this work out?" Cara's obvious worry

caused him to consider how this search for her half brother might go awry. What if she unearthed Arly Penks and the man harmed her?

"We'll both be fine," he said. "And remember what I said about the mine. Half is yours. You've earned it."

Cara's tongue slipped out a fraction as she licked her lips. Glancing left and right, she impetuously stood on tiptoe and kissed Slocum before hurrying away. The blush heightened the color in her cheeks and turned her into about the loveliest woman Slocum had ever seen.

Slocum spent the rest of the day hunting for Arly Penks. When he opened his brother Robert's watch and saw that it was almost time to meet Cara, Slocum hoped the woman had met with better luck, but he doubted it. Slocum set off toward the land office.

After twenty minutes, Slocum began to worry. When Cara hadn't shown up after a half hour, he paced back and forth in front of the brick building until he wore a trail in the wood. Slocum had not found any trace of Arly Penks, but what of Cara? She must have run into trouble. Big trouble, and Slocum had no idea how to find her.

He swung about, hand darting toward his Colt Navy when he heard quick footsteps behind him. He let out pent-up breath when he saw the dark-haired woman rushing toward him. Then the relief passed and anger replaced it.

"Where have you been? You're late."

"Why, John, you were worried," she said, teasing him. Her eyes danced, and the smile on her face was broad enough to tell him nothing he could say would bother her in the least.

"What did you find?"

"It took quite a while, but I found a man willing to speak. However, he demanded money, and I had none. My story of hunting for my lost brother carried no weight with him."

"Where is he?" Slocum's pulse raced. He wanted to find

Penks and get an accounting from him. If the gunman had murdered Happy Harry, he had done it for blood money paid by Penks.

"Across town. Please hurry, John. This is important, very important. The man does not appear to be the sort to rely on for long."

Fifteen minutes of brisk walking brought them to a small café. The smell of grease and bad food caught in Slocum's throat and made him choke. He wondered how Cara had ever screwed up her courage enough to even enter such a low-class establishment. Her need to find her brother must drive her more than Slocum had thought.

In the dim café, Slocum looked around. The men eating here had all seen better days. Some might have been railroad workers. Others sported the scars of pugilists: flattened noses and cauliflower ears. None looked to be the kind of man Cara was likely to bring home for her parents' approval.

"He told me his name was Frisco. There, that one," Cara said, pointing at a man sitting at a table near the back of the café. The man she indicated stared at her, belched, and then wiped his mouth on his grimy sleeve. Cara shuddered and moved closer to Slocum.

One man with a broken nose started to say something to Cara, then saw the expression on Slocum's face. He subsided, grumbling, having seen his own death mirrored in Slocum's cold green eyes.

"You told the lady you knew her brother," Slocum said to Frisco.

"Might," the man said, pushing his chair back. He tipped up and balanced on the back two chair legs so he could glower at Slocum. "Depends."

"On what?"

"Money. Gimme money and my memory might get better." He smiled, showing blackened teeth. The front one had been broken off. Slocum saw others had been cracked and turned green along the fracture lines.

"How'd you and Arly Penks come to know each other?" Slocum asked.

"We're friends from way back. Happened to see him here in town yesterday. Want to know more, you pay me."

Slocum's foot shot out and caught the front chair leg. He kicked hard and pulled the chair from under Frisco. The man crashed to the floor, arms flailing. Slocum stepped up and put his boot on the man's chest to hold him down.

From the corner of his eye, Slocum saw a man coming for him. He ducked, ground his heel down hard into Frisco's rib cage, then swung his fist in a short arc that ended in the attacking man's belly. Air whooshed from his lungs, and the man collapsed to the floor beside Frisco, gasping for breath.

"Anyone else thinking about taking me on?" asked Slocum. He stood stock-still, a coiled spring ready to explode. No one looking at him doubted his ability to cut them down where they stood. Quiet fell over the room. Slocum returned to the felled Frisco. He lifted his boot a half inch, the threat of returning it apparent to the trapped man.

Slocum saw no one else willing to bother him or Cara and turned his glare back on his informant.

"I don't know nuthin'!" Frisco protested. "I was just funnin' the little lady. I thought me and her might—ugh!" He groaned in pain as Slocum's heel crushed down into his diaphragm. Only when the pressure lessened did Frisco regain his breath.

"That's not what I want to hear," Slocum said. "Nothing bad about the lady or your intentions toward her. Do you know Arly Penks or not?"

"Yeah, I know him. The little weasel done me out of fifty dollars." Frisco winced when Slocum pressed down harder. "Don't do that, mister. I'm tellin' the truth. He cheated me in a card game a couple nights back. Over at the Silver Cartwheel. Ask anybody."

"We have something in common," Slocum said, easing up on the pressure a mite.

"What's that?" Frisco looked more like a trapped rat every second. Slocum knew he became that much more dangerous. Killing him or anyone in the room would only derail attempts to locate Penks.

"You want money. I want blood." Slocum heard Cara gasp but did not look her way. "Where is Penks now?"

"He left. He hightailed it out of town."

"When?"

"I dunno. I looked for him, but he was gone this morning. Might have left Carson City yesterday."

"Show him the picture, Miss Penks," Slocum said. He saw Cara moving at the edge of his vision, fumbling to pull out the picture of her half brother. She thrust it toward Frisco as if the photograph might burn her fingers.

"That the man you saw?"

"Penks is older, but it looks to be him. Yeah, that's the man who rooked me out of my money."

Slocum considered the answer. He lifted his boot from Frisco's chest and stepped back. Aside to Cara he asked, "Did you show him the picture before?"

"No, I just mentioned Arly's name. He told me about the scar when I asked for a description."

"How'd you come to know of the scar?" Slocum fixed Frisco with his cold gaze again.

"He carries a knife in a sheath in his left boot. He pulled it on me. His pants leg tore and I seen it. Danged near a foot long, that scar. All puckered and ugly pink."

"It *was* Arlin!" cried Cara.

"Where'd he go when he left town?"

Frisco shrugged and Slocum knew he had squeezed as much juice from this source as he could.

"Thanks for your help," Slocum said. He dropped a dollar bill onto Frisco's chest, then took Cara's arm and left. Only after they had left the dingy café did he hear any sound from inside. Then pandemonium broke loose as everyone cussed and shouted and demanded to know why Frisco had drawn such a dangerous man's attention to them.

"You have to be careful what you say in places like that," Slocum said. "You say anything about the scar or did Frisco mention it first?"

"I described Arly, but never said anything about the scar. Not before he spoke to you, John. You held them all at bay, as if they were a pack of rabid dogs!"

"He's left Carson City," Slocum said, disappointed. He wanted to find his former partner and have it out with him. Now he was denied that chance—for a spell. Slocum was certain his and Arly Penks's paths would cross again.

"What are we going to do?"

"Get the deed, then return to Virginia City. The Silver Jackass Mine needs protecting."

They returned to the land office next to the Wells Fargo office. Slocum considered having Cara remain outside so she wouldn't spook the clerk, then pushed the notion out of his head. She deserved to know what progress he made, and she had played fair with him.

The stout clerk looked up when Slocum came into the small office. Leaning on the counter, Slocum waited for the clerk to shuffle through the papers and come over. The man dropped his large ledger onto the counter and thumbed it open to the page with the smudged entry and two bogus quit claims.

"Afternoon," Slocum said. "What progress is there on the deed?"

"Well, sir, I got back two replies real quick. One from Arthur Conroy and another from Dr. Hanley. Upstanding citizens, both, and of good character, from my personal experience."

"So?" asked Cara. "Does this mean you will issue the new deed to Mr. Slocum?"

The clerk favored her with a smile. Cara beamed at him. Slocum doubted her good humor turned the tide, but it did not hurt.

"It'll take a day to get all the forms, but I see no reason not to issue Mr. Slocum here a full interest in that mine.

He's proved to me he's the rightful, sole surviving partner.''

"What of the man bringing in the quit claims?" Slocum tapped the open ledger on the counter and the two forged title transfers.

"Suppose it's up to me to notify the sheriff about trying to foist off on me forged documents, if he's not too busy riding the circuit and serving process." The clerk turned and spat at a hidden cuspidor. Slocum heard the brass pot ring loudly with the accurate gob.

"Don't bother," Slocum said, not wanting the law questioning him. He could deal with his own problems, once the title was clear and the copy riding high in his pocket. "No harm has been done, and I'll have full title to the mine. That ought to serve me well if there's any more trouble."

"I'll wire Sheriff Tyler down in Virginia City to let him know about the forgeries. He might be more interested than the local no-account we elected last year." The clerk spat again at the mention of the county law officer. "You can mosey back tomorrow around noon. I'll have the deed all executed legal-like then."

"Tomorrow!" exclaimed Cara.

"That will be fine. Thanks for all you've done," Slocum said, guiding the woman from the land office again.

"We have to wait until tomorrow, John! Tomorrow!"

It rankled that they had to wait, but Slocum saw a silver lining to this dark cloud. When he pointed out that they had to get a hotel room for the night, Cara's mood brightened. So did his. He never once thought of her low-down cheat of a brother until the next morning.

16

"You're mighty quiet, John. What is troubling you?" Cara Penks moved slightly on the hard wagon seat until her leg pressed firmly against his. Slocum barely noticed. His attention was fixed too firmly on the high walls of rock on either side of the road. A man standing atop either of those massive slabs of jagged gray stone could drop a pebble off and kill anyone on the road.

Slocum had seen what the Apaches did down in New Mexico Territory in places like Dog Canyon or the Navajos over in Canyon de Chelly. There weren't Indians on the loose in the Comstock, but there might be a worse enemy: Arly Penks.

"Just tuckered out," Slocum said, telling a half-truth. The night spent with Cara had been anything but relaxing. They had made love, collapsed in exhaustion, and then gone at it like minks in heat all over again.

"I am, too," she confided, resting her head on his shoulder. "And I want to do it again tonight." Her dark hair fluttered up in the wind and tickled his nose. Slocum moved slightly on the wagon seat to keep a clear view of the road and the cliffs above.

"We have to reach Virginia City first," Slocum said, eyes darting from one rocky crag to the other. "We'll have at least one night on the road. This wagon can't go much faster, and old Vic is wearing down with every mile."

"There's no reason we can't enjoy each other's company on the trail," she said, her hand running up and down his arm, tracing the thick muscles of his biceps and upper shoulder.

She pulled back when he sat straighter and his hand moved toward the six-shooter in his cross-draw holster.

"What's wrong?"

Slocum squinted into the sun to get some idea if he was spooked over a bird or if a man had silhouetted himself against the cloudless blue sky. Swinging around and craning his neck, Slocum peered straight up the sheer wall. A loud cawing echoed down to him and a crow with a three-foot wingspan swooped low, saw there was nothing eat, and surged back into the sky with powerful flaps of its wings.

"Jumpy," Slocum said. "Have been since leaving Carson City."

"You're worried we might be ambushed?" Cara sat with her hands in her lap, folded as if she sat in church listening to a sermon. "Do you think Arlin would harm us?"

"Arly Penks would *kill* us in a split second," Slocum said with some bitterness. "No reflection on you or your other kin, but Penks tried to kill me once—and murdered our partner." That part bothered Slocum the most. Partners stuck together, no matter what. One never murdered a partner. Ever. That was as bad as shooting an unarmed man.

"You can't be certain, John. That man who kidnapped me—the gunman with the silver conchos. You claimed he shot your partner and set the fires in Virginia City."

"He was working for someone. I feel it in my bones. And I saw him talking to a man at the stables."

"That might have been anyone," Cara pointed out. "You said you never caught a clear view of him."

Slocum shrugged. What she said was true. He might be jumping at ghosts that did not exist. Still, he had come to believe in his sixth sense telling him if he rode into danger. It had kept him alive more than once. And a quick glance up at the left cliff confirmed his worst fear.

"Rockslide!" Slocum yelled. He snapped the reins hard against the jackass's rump to get the animal trotting along. When it refused to move any faster, Slocum grabbed Cara's arm and jerked her out of the wagon. They hit the ground hard.

"John, wait, I can't get my feet under me."

Slocum never gave her a chance. He scooped her up in his arms and started running back down the road in the direction of Carson City. For a few seconds Cara struggled, then calmed. Slocum's speed picked up and then the earth rumbled as the rocks crashed down into the road. A flying piece of stone clipped Slocum in the shoulder and spun him around.

A cloud of dust billowed forth and choked him. Slocum lost his balance and fell back heavily, Cara on top of him. A new wave of thunder signaled a second avalanche tumbling rock into the road. With a hard twist, Slocum threw Cara to the ground and rolled so he could protect her with his body.

Groaning under the impact of heavier rock, Slocum remained over the woman until the dust got so heavy he could not bear it another second. Coughing, choking, he pulled his bandanna to his nose and mouth in an effort to breathe. He didn't have to ask if Cara was all right. She fought to get free from under him. Slocum pulled up to his knees and let her scramble away.

"John," she rasped through a dirt-filled mouth. "We were almost killed!"

"Reckon the donkey finally found a reason to gallop," Slocum said. He saw the remains of the wagon poking out from under a tumble of rock. The jackass stood on the far side of the rockfall, braying loudly in fear.

"How can you be as cool as a cucumber and make jokes? Oh!" She stood and brushed dirt off her dress, creating a new dust storm.

"This isn't the first time I've had a brush with death," Slocum reminded her. "If my luck holds, it won't be the last. Only when my luck gives out will I end up *under* a cairn of rocks."

Together they picked their way through the rock until they reached the donkey. The jackass brayed angrily and tried to buck when Slocum helped Cara onto its back, but the animal settled down to a steady walk, happy to be relieved of the burden of pulling the heavy wagon.

Slocum walked beside the jackass, keeping the bridle in hand. He saw that Cara was deep in thought, pondering how close she had come to being crushed under the avalanche. Slocum turned and studied the high cliffs on either side of the now blocked road and wondered if he had seen a man above them or if it had been nothing more than his imagination. If Cara had not been with him, he would have hiked to the top of the cliff and looked for traces of a would-be killer.

For the two days it took them to return to Virginia City, Slocum felt eyes boring into his back. And every time he looked, no one was there.

"I am bushed, John," Cara Penks told him. "I feel as if I can sleep for twenty years. And hungry! I could eat an entire cow. And then sleep."

Slocum smiled. He felt the same way after the long walk into Virginia City. There had been little food along the way since he had decided to keep traveling rather than stop to hunt. A passing rider had shared some jerky with them, but other than water and a few tubers and berries he had found, they had eaten no substantial food.

"I can stand a hot bath," Slocum said. "And food, too. You get a room, and I'll see you to dinner later."

"What?" She stared at him with her eyes wide. "Aren't you coming up right away?"

"I have some business to tend to," Slocum said. He touched the deed resting in his pocket. The walk back had given him time to think about returning to the Silver Jackass and the tons of silver begging to be ripped from the rock—and the hard work that would take. Better to sell the mine and use the money to move on.

"The mine," she said, seeing how his fingers drummed on the deed. "You have decided to sell it?"

"There's no time like the present," Slocum said. "I can get a good price. You don't need to worry on that count."

"I'm not worried, John. You're an honest man, an honorable gentleman. You'll do what is best." Cara paused and then started to say something more. She clamped her mouth shut without another word, but Slocum knew what was on her mind: her half brother.

In that they shared a profound interest. Slocum had a score to settle with Arly Penks.

"Rest up. I may be a while finding the right buyer."

"All right, John." Cara looked around furtively, then gave him a quick kiss. With this, she spun and hurried into the hotel. It took all of Slocum's willpower not to follow her. Selling the Silver Jackass Mine could wait.

Finding Arly Penks could not. Slocum felt pressure mounting on him to locate the renegade miner and bring him to justice. Sheriff Tyler might be interested in Penks's activities, but there was no proof. That had died with the gunman Slocum had cut down. The land clerk in Carson City might testify how Penks had tried to pass off forged quit claims, but even if convicted, this would not mete out the proper punishment for all the man had done.

"Harry, I promise he won't get away with killing you." Slocum settled his gun belt and started off for K Street to check each saloon in turn for any sign of their errant partner. He gave up hunting for Penks when he poked his head into the Deep Shaft Saloon's front door and was greeted by the three miners he and Happy Harry had saved.

"Hey, Slocum, come on in. Let us buy you a drink. We're celebratin'!" called Mike McDermont. The man still wore splints on his leg, but the expression of exultation told Slocum something good had happened to him and his two partners. From the pie-eyed condition of Lew Blasko and Bob Ed Briggs, it was something *really* good.

"What's the occasion?" Slocum asked, seating himself at the table with the three miners. Lew Blasko slapped him on the back. Slocum forced himself not to wince since the man was in such good spirits and obviously not malicious in his regard.

"We struck the mother lode. I do declare, it's wider than a mile!" cried Bob Ed Briggs. He threw his arms wide to show how much silver they had discovered and fell heavily to floor. He lay there laughing until McDermont pulled him back up.

"The Croaking Frog's been renamed the Roaring Bull-frog," Bob Ed declared. "There's nothing piddly-little in *that* mine. We're rich, filthy rich!"

"Congratulations," Slocum said. "What are you planning on doing with your newfound fortune?"

"Gold Hill," whispered Mike McDermont in a hoarse voice. "We're building houses up there among all the rich folks."

"There's good property to be had at a cheap price," Slocum allowed. Visions of the flames leaping sky-high came to haunt him. "Half of Gold Hill burned down and ought to be for sale cheap."

"That forger's house, you mean?" Lew Blasko knocked back a shot of whiskey and motioned to the barkeep for more. "We don't want a small place like that."

"Forger's house?" Slocum came around, immediately alert. "What do you mean?"

"That's where the fire started what burned down half the houses. Ol' Benny Pendleton brought it on himself, with his inks and solvents. Why he spilled so much kerosene is beyond me. The sheriff claims Pendleton was responsible for half of all the bad claims and counterfeit money in the Comstock. Don't know about that," said Blasko. "Do know we want *big* houses, not piddly-little ones like Pendleton had."

Another piece of the puzzle fit together. The silver-concho bedecked gunman had set fire to Pendleton's house to cover the forged quit claims—or Arly Penks had done it. Slocum knew this was wild speculation, but it fit the facts.

"You sound as if you intend to stay in Virginia City," Slocum said. "Most mine owners want to sell when they hit it rich and move on."

"We're gonna sell stock and make big money, yes, sir," piped up McDermont. He cocked his head to one side and peered at Slocum. "You sound like a man wanting out of his claim. Is the Silver Jackass Mine for sale?"

This triggered a round of spirited debate among the men about acquiring a new property. Slocum put the deed and assay reports on the table in front of him and let them argue the merit of taking on another hole in the ground, even one with the promise of so much silver. He drank slowly while the three drank one shot of whiskey after another. And in the end, Slocum had sold his mine to the trio for $50,000.

"A hard bargain, Slocum, but one we all profit from. We'll have our banker draw up the check in the morning," Blasko said.

"Hell, Lew," said Briggs. "We'll have our *bank* do it. We got the money. Let's the buy the friggin' bank, too!"

This set them off on another round of arguments over how to spend their money. Slocum listened to how they'd buy the race track and the general store, all the saloons in town, including the Deep Shaft. He steered them back to the matter of the Silver Jackass and got a scratchy outline of terms scribbled on the back of an envelope someone found on the floor.

"See you gents in the morning over at the bank," Slocum said.

"We'll be there, Slocum. You drive a hard bargain, but your mine's worth it. And we all feel an obligation to you for what you and Happy Harry done for us."

"You're robbing me blind, McDermont," Slocum shot back, smiling. "The Silver Jackass is worth more than $50,000 and we all know it."

"Of course we all know it, Slocum. That's why we're stinkin' rich now!" Blasko proclaimed. This produced new laughter and more boasting. Slocum slipped from the saloon and into the Virginia City night. Cold wind whipped from the tall peaks, but somehow tonight the breeze felt invigorating rather than freezing.

He was richer by $25,000. He might have made that much from the mine in a few months, but Slocum had the increasing feeling of wanderlust. He had to move on and see new horizons. The mountains closed in on him and Virginia City had lost its novelty. Everything new and fresh now seemed tawdry and even tiresome.

Slocum started back for the hotel to tell Cara of the impending sale. Although the three miners might be drunk now, Slocum knew they would not forget the deal. He had the agreement in his pocket, along with the deed to the Silver Jackass Mine. The witnesses to the agreement were myriad and the miners had reputations for being honest men.

Besides that, they were getting a mine worth ten times what they paid for it. None of the three was a dullard, and now that rivers of silver poured from the Croaking Frog— Roaring Bullfrog—they could afford to expand their financial empire.

Slocum whistled softly to himself as he walked briskly, but his pace slowed when the same sensation he had experienced on the road to Virginia City returned to trouble him.

Reaching to his left side, Slocum slipped the leather

thong off the hammer of his six-shooter. Never slowing, he kept walking, then suddenly ducked and dodged into an alley. From behind he heard the hard pounding of boots against the crushed quartz ore in the street. Slocum whipped out his six-gun and waited for someone to show himself in the mouth of the alley. When no one presented himself as a target, Slocum knew he was the prey and had not merely imagined someone was after him.

Slocum dashed to the far end of the alley and peered around the corner of a building—and almost got his face blown off. The shotgun ripped away most of the wood and sent splinters flying into his face. Slocum reacted instinctively. His six-shooter came up, and he fired. He heard Arly Penks yelp in fright and saw the man take off running like a frightened rabbit.

Brushing the sharp wood fragments from his face, Slocum ran after the fleeing man, but Penks proved fleeter of foot. Slocum got off two more shots at Penks's back. Both slugs went wide of their target. Slocum cursed when he saw the result. He had not slowed the man's escape. If anything, the shots hastened the man's retreat.

Penks cut around a corner and vanished down one street. By the time Slocum got around the building to stand in the middle of the broad street, he knew he had lost his quarry. Arly Penks was nowhere to be seen.

17

Slocum paused to reload, then settled down to a serious search for Arly Penks. He asked in saloons and hunted the back ways of Virginia City but could not unearth the back-shooting son of a bitch. In disgust, Slocum walked to the middle of busy C Street and looked up and down, thinking he might catch sight of Penks.

Nothing. The ground had opened up and swallowed him.

"It ought to have swallowed him when the explosion went off in the mine," grumbled Slocum. To his way of thinking, the wrong man had died after the Silver Jackass had been destroyed. It ought to be Happy Harry and Slocum and Penks's half sister sharing in the silver bounty.

As Cara's name brushed across his mind, Slocum went cold inside.

"Cara!" He spun and ran as hard as he could for the hotel where she had gone to rent a room. Slocum hadn't been thinking clearly, and now this failing might have come home to haunt him. In Carson City, he had made no secret of being with Cara. And on the road back to Virginia City, he had worried that someone watched them.

The rockfall suddenly turned into an attempt to kill them

both—and Arly Penks was the likely culprit. Penks knew his half sister was back in Virginia City and was hindering his attempts to forge his way into complete ownership of the Silver Jackass Mine.

Slocum, out of breath, crashed through the front doors and into the hotel lobby. Panting harshly, he turned to the desk clerk. The man's eyes were wide and his complexion pale. Something had frightened him badly before Slocum's sudden entrance.

"Where is she? Cara Penks," Slocum rasped out.

"S-she, she's gone," the man stammered. "He took her. Said he was her brother and that he was lookin' after her honor, that you and her, that you dishonored her, that you—"

"Penks," snarled Slocum. "Was it Arly Penks? Do you remember seeing me with my two partners?"

"That was his name. I heard her call him Arlin. Then she wasn't sayin' much. He kept her on a close leash. S-said you and h-her, that you—"

"Where'd he take her?" The coldness in Slocum's request caused the man to turn even paler and to tremble.

"Cain't tell you. He said he'd k-kill me if I did. Wanted to regain her honor, he s-said."

With one smooth movement, Slocum had his six-shooter out, cocked and aimed directly into the man's face.

"He might kill you if you tell me, but if you don't, I swear I *will.*" There wasn't a tremor in the gun barrel. Slocum knew the clerk saw only the gradual whitening of the knuckle as his finger tightened on the six-gun's hair trigger.

"B-back to your mine. That's what he said." From the sweat beading on the clerk's forehead, Slocum knew he was too scared to lie. But that didn't mean Penks hadn't left the lie to be passed along.

"How do you come to know?" Slocum asked.

"He said. I overheard him sayin' it to his half sister."

"Is there anywhere around Virginia City he might go to roost?"

"I don't know him, Mr. Slocum. Honest, I don't. Other than—"

"Other than where?" Slocum prompted. He didn't lessen the tension on the trigger. If the clerk didn't speak quickly, he'd have a new hole drilled smack-dab between his eyes.

"Heard tell he had a place up in Gold Hill. Him and another gent. Don't know the names. Please, Mr. S-Slocum, I'm tellin' the gospel truth!"

Slocum relaxed his finger and let down the hammer on his Colt. He was boiling inside but kept a cold exterior. His mind raced. There was no way he could go through Gold Hill hunting for Penks and hope to find him. The richest of the rich lived up there and might not take kindly to a manhunt in their midst. But someone who might know about Penks and any crony walked about Virginia City.

"Is Sheriff Tyler back from riding the circuit?" Slocum asked.

The clerk nodded, relieved at not having the gun pointed at his face any longer. "Over in his office, last I saw."

Slocum stalked out, making a beeline for the sheriff's office. The light burned in the window, and Slocum hoped it was Tyler inside and not one of his deputies. He paused in the doorway and saw the lawman sitting behind a battered desk, adding up a column of figures.

"What you want, Slocum? I got work that's killing me by inches. Too danged many pieces of paper to file away. I swear, I spend more time writin' than I do catchin' crooks."

"Did the state land clerk wire you?"

"What? Oh, yeah, I got it somewhere. Came this morning. Seems he's spun quite a tale of forging and thought I'd be interested. Don't see how, though. Not with Pendleton dead."

"The house that was set on fire. Are you sure Pendleton died in the fire?"

"Sure as anything," Tyler said. "What's your interest?"

Slocum almost told him how Penks had kidnapped his half sister, but something made him hold back. He wasn't sure, but it might have been nothing more than simple vengeance. He wanted revenge on Penks for all he had done.

"Did Pendleton have any other hangouts up in Gold Hill? I heard he had more than one place."

Tyler scratched his head. "Might have. He was busy as a beaver with his pen and ink. He wasn't a very good forger from all accounts, but he didn't have to be around here since most folks can't do more 'n write their own names. He might have got himself another place, but Doc Hanley is sure it was Pendleton who died in the fire."

"Anyone ever see Penks and Pendleton together?"

"Not that I recollect, but then Penks was never too sociable. What are you sayin', Slocum?"

"Might be they are one and the same. Penks is going to a whale of a lot of trouble to cover his trail. If he's been forging documents, too, he might want a summer name to cover that."

"Pendleton?" Tyler shook his head. "Slocum, it's way too late to be spinning these wild yarns of yours. Go get some sleep. With that filly you've been squiring around, I'm sure you can think of something better to do than bend my ear." Tyler turned back to the numbers. His lips moved and he chewed on a pencil as he worked to add up a new column.

Slocum left, his steps turning toward Gold Hill. It took him a half hour to reach the house where the fire had started. Only charred timbers remained. Slocum poked through the ruins and saw nothing to show that anyone had been there recently. Still, he had the feeling he was close to finding Penks.

The sun poked up for a new day before Slocum sat on the side of the road, about ready to admit defeat. Then he saw a small knot of boys running down the road, laughing and shoving each other. He waved to them. They approached cautiously, not sure what he wanted from them.

"What do you know of yonder house?" Slocum asked, pointing to the ruins of Pendleton's house.

"That's where Mr. Pendleton lived," ventured one young boy. "We didn't have nothing to do with the fire, mister. But it was big one!"

"I know. I saw it," Slocum said. "You ever see Pendleton with any friends?"

"Sure," said another. But a third elbowed him to silence.

"What are you after, mister?" The third boy was the obvious leader.

"I'm looking for Pendleton's friends," Slocum said. He reached into his pocket and pulled out the wad of greenbacks he had taken from the black-clad gunman. Then he knew something better to offer as a bribe. He fished out three silver conchos and let them catch the sun so they reflected into the boys' eyes.

"Those are just like the ones worn by that gunfighter Mr. Pendleton was always talking to," piped up one.

"Where'd you get 'em, mister?" asked the ringleader.

Slocum flipped him one. "You might say I found them. They weren't much use anymore to their owner. You see Pendleton talking with another man?" He described Arly Penks.

"Sure, we saw the three of them together a lot. Always sneaking around, pulling down shades inside as if anyone cared to spy on them."

"You'd never do a thing like that, would you?" Slocum tossed a second concho to the smallest of the boys. "Not here or the other place Pendleton had."

"Neither place, mister. Really," said the leader. His eyes shot down the road to a ramshackle place.

"That the one where Penks went?" Slocum fingered the last concho. The boy who had not gotten one was itching to speak. It took only a few seconds of indecision for the rush of information Slocum wanted.

"Sure is." The boy waited for Slocum to toss him the

last concho. He studied it carefully, then looked up. "These look exactly like the ones that gunfighter wore. Where'd you get 'em, mister?"

"Might be a spot of blood on them. You'd better check," Slocum said, getting to his feet. His eyes fixed on the old house at the end of the lane. Around the back he saw a horse working at a pile of hay, but other than this, he saw no trace of anyone in the area.

The boys backed away, then ran off whispering among themselves. Slocum knew his parting comment about the conchos would keep them buzzing all day long. He made his way through the debris of the fire. The wind had blown the flames away from the house at the end of the street, saving a house about ready to collapse under its own weight.

A mine shaft sank into the mountain not fifty feet from the house. The entire area was festooned with holes and old mines cut by the first prospectors. A few had turned into rich mines but had played out years ago. The newest discoveries were all down the hill, at the edges of Virginia City and beyond. Slocum's gaze kept returning to the mine shaft. He wondered if Penks used that as an escape route or if he might hold his sister prisoner there.

With the sunlight beaming down, it would be impossible for Slocum to sneak up unseen to the house. Yet he hesitated to wait a full day until nightfall. Penks would be getting mighty antsy about moving on now that all his plans had fallen apart.

Slocum tried to reconstruct what had gone on with Arly Penks. He and the gunman were obviously in cahoots. And the forger, Pendleton, worked with them. A falling-out might account for the gunman—or Penks—killing Pendleton. Or maybe the forger had outlived his usefulness and presented a danger. Penks had gone out of his way to make it seem that he had died in the Silver Jackass Mine explosion. Pendleton could testify differently and might have been imprudent enough to let the treacherous miner know.

However they had planned it, Slocum and Harlan had to end up dead so there would be no one to dispute the bogus claim for the Silver Jackass.

Walking slowly, Slocum picked his way through the burned-out buildings and finally came to the field stretching all the way to the tumbledown house. He could never cross such a long stretch of open ground unseen. If Penks waited for him, Slocum would be an easy target. But the pressure of time wore down heavier by the second on Slocum's shoulders. Cara was in danger. Her brother had dragged her from the hotel to this desolate spot, either to kill her outright or to lure Slocum here so both Cara and Slocum could be eliminated.

Cutting away from the house, Slocum went to the steep slope of the mountain rising behind the house. He edged along the rocky terrain until he came to the mine shaft. Listening hard for any sound, he heard only the distant creaking of timbers. He saw some scuff marks telling that someone had entered the mine recently, but the hard rock floor didn't take kindly to tracks. Slocum couldn't tell if the man had left or if he might have had a hostage with him.

Slocum slipped into the mouth of the mine, examining the timbers above his head. The wood had seen better days. From the aging, he guessed this might have been one of the first mines cut into the hillside. He took a few wary steps, every sense straining. When his toe whacked against a box, Slocum stopped and knelt.

"Miner's black fuse," he said, pulling a foot-long piece from the wood crate. Holding it up to peer at it in the dim light filtering in from the mouth of the mine, Slocum saw the end had been cut recently. Penks had taken another piece out of the mine with him.

And Slocum thought he knew what the miner intended on doing. He dropped the fuse and hurried outside into the fresh air and bright light. His eyes fixed on the house a hundred feet away. It might be suicidal, but Slocum saw no alternative. Using what little cover there was, he made his way toward the back of the house.

His heart was about ready to explode by the time he reached the back door. It had been pulled off one hinge and hung at a crazy angle, and in the dust on the kitchen floor beyond, Slocum saw distinct footprints. Freshly made prints from boots marched alongside a woman's smaller foot.

Slocum clutched his Colt Navy and stepped into the cramped kitchen. His nose wrinkled at the heavy odor of kerosene that hit him like a bludgeon. Gallons had been poured onto anything wood in the kitchen and small pools remained on the floor. Slocum stepped over the puddles of volatile kerosene and moved into a dining room.

Dust lay everywhere and this room, too, had been drenched with kerosene. A single spark would send the entire house up in a blaze that could never be put out until only ashes remained. Slocum moved through a deathtrap laid by Arly Penks.

And he had no idea where the man might be.

Slocum pressed his ear against the doorjamb. Far-off thumping noises were all he could detect. They might come from the second floor, but he could not be sure. Cautiously exploring, Slocum checked every room on the ground floor for any sign of Arly Penks or his sister.

"Cara," he called softly. "Are you there?" The thumping sound grew louder. It definitely came from upstairs. But before Slocum took a single step onto the stairs, he examined the steps. It wasn't beyond Arly Penks's cunning mind to booby-trap the steps to catch any unwary rescuer.

Slocum found himself more worried than ever when he found no trap other than the entire kerosene-doused house. He slowly mounted the steps and entered a small corridor. Four shut doors arrayed in a semicircle at the end presented the next challenge for him.

Slocum dropped to his hands and knees and peered under the first door. He caught no sign of movement inside. He went to the next door and saw moving shadows. Rather than enter, he checked the other two rooms. Two shadows restlessly swayed to and fro in the last room. Slocum got to his feet, clutched his six-gun in his hand, and slowly turned the cut-glass doorknob to this room.

The door yielded with a creaking protest of swelled wood. When it stuck halfway open, Slocum turned and rammed his shoulder against it. He spilled into the room, six-shooter ready for action.

He found himself aiming his Colt at curtains flapping in the wind coming through broken window panes. The room was empty. Slocum sped back to the other room, the first one where he had detected small movement.

This door was locked. He wasted no time trying to figure out an easy way in. He had already betrayed himself to Arly Penks, should the man be listening. Slocum kicked like a mule and the door exploded inward. It smashed against a wall and rebounded, but Slocum was already halfway into the room, his six-shooter preceding him.

He saw Cara Penks securely tied to the head of a brass bed that had partially fallen to the floor. She struggled against the ropes holding her and tried desperately to say something through the gag in her mouth.

Before Slocum released her, he went to a wardrobe and jerked open the door, expecting to find Penks inside with a drawn gun. Only tattered clothing and a cloud of dust and moths rushed out to greet him. He swung around, hunting for someone to shoot.

Almost reluctantly, he holstered his six-shooter and dropped to one knee to free Cara.

He started working on the ropes cruelly cutting into her wrists, but she kicked at him and thrashed about.

"What's wrong? Don't you want me to untie you?" He saw her eyes go wide, then anger rush to replace a flash of fear. She tried to shout past the dirty rag fastened into her mouth, and Slocum knew what was bothering her most.

"This what you want out?"

He pulled the gag from her mouth. Cara choked and

almost retched. Then she looked up and shouted at him, "We have to get out of here. Arlin knew you'd come. He's going to kill us both!"

"I reckoned he had some plan in mind," Slocum said, fumbling at the ropes binding her wrists. "But I haven't seen hide nor hair of him."

"Outside, John, he is waiting outside. The entire house is a death trap!"

Slocum heard a hissing sound outside and rushed to the window. Below he saw Arly Penks applying a lucifer to the end of a short length of the miner's black fuse. It sizzled and popped and began to burn at its one foot per minute speed.

Slocum went cold inside when he realized the decision facing him. He had less than a minute to free Cara before the entire kerosene-doused house exploded. Or he could leave her and save himself.

Faster than thought, Slocum whipped out his six-shooter and got off a shot at Arly Penks. The slug missed by inches. Penks ran from the house, ducking and dodging as Slocum fired repeatedly at him. The treacherous miner let out an ugly laugh when it was obvious Slocum could not hit him, then ducked behind an overturned wagon. He poked his head up to watch his deadly handiwork. When Slocum's Colt Navy came up empty, he realized there wasn't any way in hell he could drive Penks from hiding before the fuse burned to its end and ignited the house.

Slocum looked at the woman struggling on the bed and then back out where her half brother crouched, waiting for his lethal firebomb to explode. Slocum had to make a quick decision. Untying the woman might take more time than remained on the fuse, and even if he got her free, they had to get down the stairs and outside before the fire engulfed them.

Then Slocum knew he had waited too long. A sound like

someone gasping rushed up the stairs. Behind the sound came a wall of heat and flame. The death house had been set afire, trapping both Cara Penks and John Slocum on the second floor.

18

Slocum slammed the door to keep the heat from blistering his face. The floor under his boots already sagged and smoldered as the kerosene-fed blaze spread with voracious speed.

"John, please!" pleaded Cara. She fought to get free, but Slocum knew there was no way he could untie her bonds before the entire house vanished in a cauldron of flames, with both of them in the deadly center.

He shoved his six-shooter into his holster and reached out. With a tremendous jerk, he pulled the brass rail at the head of the bed free. Cara was still tied to it, but Slocum didn't care. He shoved his shoulder into her midriff as she tried to stand. Knocking her back onto the mattress prevented her from struggling for a moment. Slocum's arms engulfed the thin mattress and he lifted.

Twisting fast, he heaved Cara, brass rail, and mattress out the window. Never hesitating, he followed. He fell through the air and tried to jerk about so he wouldn't land atop the woman. He failed. His weight crushed the air from her lungs. They lay on the mattress for a moment, gasping for breath.

Then breathing became even more difficult. A blanket of superheated air rushed from the house and covered them like a suffocating blanket. Slocum tried to protect the helpless woman the best he could with his body. He felt the flesh on his back blistering, adding to the pain already there. Then his tattered shirt exploded in flames from the intense heat billowing from the house. The mattress spat tiny flames wherever cinders and burning splinters fell.

"John," gasped Cara. "What happened?"

"We've got to get away," he panted. He tried to pick her up, but his strength failed him. Slocum staggered and landed on her again. His hands closed around the brass rail. It was turning hot to the touch, but he did not abandon it. Digging in as if he engaged in a tug-of-war, he started pulling.

At first Cara slid along easily, the mattress beneath her. Then the mattress shredded away and he had to pull her on the rocky ground. He shut his ears to her shrieking protest. She might be cut up, but if they remained close to the fire, they would be fried in seconds. Slocum noted how the brass rail cut through the ropes, but he dared not stop and encourage this by sawing on Cara's bonds. Before he had gone another ten feet, the ropes parted and he fell headlong.

Casting aside the brass bed rail, he crawled on hands and knees back to her. She lay stunned. His arm circled her waist and drew her to her feet. She stumbled, but with his help managed to stagger away from the burning house. In the distance, over the ear-splitting roar of the kerosene-fed fire, he heard the Monumental Engine Company No. 6 bell clanging mournfully.

"Water," Cara gasped.

"Later," Slocum said. "When we get farther away." But the woman pulled from his weakened grasp. Then he saw what she had already noticed. A watering trough half filled with muddy water might provide a moment's respite from the heat. Cara flopped facedown into the trough. Slocum was only a half step behind. They barely fit in the narrow trough, but the cooling water soothed his back and put out the tiny fires erupting on their clothing.

Slocum flopped like a fish out of the trough and onto the ground, getting muddy in the process. He sat up and looked around for Arly Penks, worried that the bushwhacking claim jumper might be drawing a bead on them. But Cara's half brother was nowhere to be seen. Slocum took the opportunity to dry off his six-shooter and reload.

By the time he finished, Cara pulled herself from the trough. Her wrists bled from the ropes, and she was scratched and burned in a dozen visible places. Slocum guessed she sported burns and cuts in places he couldn't see.

"My own brother," she said, amazed. "He tried to kill us. He tried to kill *me!*"

"Not the first time," Slocum said. "Unless I miss my guess, he caused the rockslide on the road back to Virginia City. And even that wasn't the first time he tried to murder me."

"He bragged to me all he had done. He . . . he's nothing but a claim jumper! He and someone named Concho were partners. They went around killing miners and stealing their claims. This was the first time—with you and Harry Harlan—he tried to kill you and use that Pendleton person to forge the claim."

"What was his game?" Slocum asked. "He faked his own death. How was he going to profit from that?"

"Concho—who was he?"

"The gunman," Slocum said. "We may never know his real name, and it doesn't much matter. He will burn in hell, no matter what he calls himself."

"Concho was supposed to pass himself off as Arlin's brother."

"But you came along," Slocum said to Cara. "You showed up and were a legitimate relative. He had to try something different. Maybe that's when he decided to bluff his way through it with forged quit claims and go to Carson City. He dropped all pretense of being dead, but it was too late.''

"The undertaker had already informed the state land clerk of his death," Cara went on. "And we were there asking for clear title to the mine. Me coming to Virginia City certainly ruined his plans."

"That was only part of it," Slocum said grimly. "It turned out I didn't kill as easy as Penks or Concho thought." He stood on shaky legs. The volunteer firemen struggled to get up the hill to the end of the lane with their steam engine pump. Not that it mattered much, since the house was already a ruin.

"They can take care of you," Slocum told the disheveled woman. "I've got business with your brother."

"He's no kin of mine," she said bitterly. "Blood is supposed to be thicker than water. He tried to *kill* me. He tried to burn me up in that house!" Cara's voice rose shrilly as shock set in. She hadn't panicked before, but now the realization of all she had endured sank in. He put his arm around her shoulders and guided her toward the fire captain.

"Slocum, you here already? You are a goldurned sight," Captain Chambers said, pushing his leather helmet back on his forehead. He ducked as something inside the house exploded and sent a cascade of fiery splinters raining down all around him. "You and the lady all right?"

"She's shaken up," Slocum said. "We were inside the house."

Chambers eyed Cara's bloody wrists and the way Slocum's back had blistered.

"Maybe I ought to get Sheriff Tyler," the volunteer fireman said uneasily.

"A good idea. Cara can explain what happened. And while you take care of her, I have an errand to run."

"John, no. Let the sheriff deal with him." Cara saw

Slocum's expression and knew that arguing with him was futile. Slocum had a score to settle and wasn't likely to let the law put Arly Penks in jail when a bullet was merited.

"I know one thing, Slocum," spoke up Chambers. The fireman looked uneasily at the house. "That wood had to be soaked in kerosene, from the smell. And the way it is spreading puts the whole area in danger."

"There aren't any houses nearby," Slocum said, but his voice trailed off when he saw the real danger. The dry grass had caught, and the fire spread rapidly. In Kansas he has seen prairie fires that burned hundreds of miles and for days on end. The sky had turned black from the smoke, and the earth took months to recover. Already around him small animals came from their burrows and sought safer ground.

"We're not even trying to put that fire out," Chambers said, jerking his thumb in the direction of the house. "We're spraying down the ground to keep the grass from carrying the fire all over town. Gold Hill's had about all it can stand these past few weeks."

"Penks," snarled Slocum, more determined than ever. "He set the other fire to kill a forger named Pendleton. And his partner, a gunman called Concho, probably set the fire at the registrar's office and gunned down Happy Harry. Concho is dead, and Arly Penks will be, soon enough. That will take care of your epidemic of fires."

"Slocum, wait!" called the fire captain, but Slocum was already heading back toward the watering trough.

Slocum dunked himself until his clothing was again saturated with the dirty water, then he set off to find Penks. The man had hidden behind an overturned wagon, but Slocum couldn't get close enough to find the man's tracks. The heat kept him at bay, and even if he had gotten closer, the wagon was charred and masked any spoor Penks might have left.

His sharp eyes searched for the most likely trail Penks

would have taken. There were only a couple places his former partner could have run to shield himself from the intense heat from the fire he had started.

A carriage house was partially burned, and Slocum doubted Penks had headed there for safety. He still had to check it out to be certain. Jumping around grass fires, Slocum dashed to the carriage house. He almost entered but held back at the last moment when he heard ominous creaking sounds from the support timbers.

A blizzard of fiery motes erupted from the building, barely missing Slocum. He ducked low and made his way forward on his belly. The carriage house wasn't on fire, but the heat had caused nails to pop from the wood and weakened the roof. Its collapse had caused the gush of coals that had almost blinded Slocum.

"Come on out, Penks," Slocum called, waiting for any hint of movement in the destroyed building. Nothing moved. Nothing.

Slocum scooted closer and scanned the various lumps and piles inside, trying to decide if Arly Penks lay dead under any of them. The bullet that ripped along the ground in front of him convinced Slocum that Penks wasn't inside. Rolling to his side, he pulled his six-shooter and tried to get off a shot.

"Where are you, Penks?" Slocum called. The man was nowhere to be seen. The bullet had not been a figment of his imagination, though. Slocum rolled onto his back and twisted so he faced the most likely hiding place for a sniper. He held his six-gun ready for immediate response, but he might as well have been the only person in the Comstock.

Getting his feet under him, Slocum crouched, then jumped forward, running as hard as he could. No new bullet sought his flesh. He reached a boulder poking up at the far side of the fenced property and used it for shelter.

"You can't get away, Penks," Slocum called, trying to draw out the renegade. "The firemen know all about you, and Sheriff Tyler is on his way with his deputies. Give it up now, or they'll gun you down.''

"What's my choice, Slocum?" came Penk's frightened voice. "You cut me down or the sheriff catches me and saves me for a necktie party. If I kill you, I get away scot-free.''

"Your sister's still alive. She won't let this rest, Penks. She'll make sure the law tracks you down, no matter how far you run.''

This produced two more slugs that ricocheted off the rock. Slocum homed in on Penks's hiding place. He saw danger heading toward the man and considered not warning him.

"Penks, the fire you set! It's heading your way. The grass is burning and will fry you good!''

Slocum hoped the warning would flush his quarry. It didn't. But he heard the pounding of heavy footsteps. Chancing a quick look around the boulder, Slocum saw that the only escape open to Penks lay down the hill toward the mine shaft. He rested his six-shooter against the rock to steady it and bided his time. Penks had to break from cover if he sought refuge in the mine.

Slocum's finger came back smoothly, and his six-gun bucked almost before he realized Penks had come into view. The fleeing claim jumper stumbled and grabbed his leg. Penks turned and fired wildly in Slocum's direction, all the bullets going wide. Slocum tried to hit the man a second time, but smoke from the grass fire blew between them and obscured his aim. Slocum fired repeatedly anyway, hoping one slug would hit Penks and end his putrid life.

Before venturing from his safe harbor, Slocum reloaded. As he rose, he choked on the heavy smoke lying like a fog over the hillside. The volunteer firemen hosed down the grass and caused the black smoke as the grass smoldered. Slocum ran toward the mine shaft, knowing

Penks couldn't see him any better than Slocum could see his quarry.

The grass burned at Slocum's ankles as he danced along the trail leading to the mine. He listened hard, but did not hear any sound of Penks blundering ahead of him. When he reached the spot where Penks had stopped, Slocum saw the bloody trail. From the amount of blood, Slocum knew he might have hit a major artery in Penk's leg.

"Give it up, Penks. You're wounded bad. You need Doc Hanley tending your leg."

His answer was an errant bullet. Slocum pressed on, choking in the heavy pall hanging over the mountainside. Slocum pressed his back against cold rock and winced when he reached the opening of the mine. Firing a couple rounds into the mine sent lead screaming into the depths.

"You're trapped, Penks. Surrender. I won't gun you down."

"Liar!" shouted Penks. His voice echoed enough to let Slocum know his quarry had gone deep into the mine shaft. "You'd shoot me in the back. You and that whore of a sister." He fired several more times.

Slocum knew Penks had gone deeper into the mine, making it more difficult to ferret him out. Choking, eyes watering, Slocum started into the mine when he heard Captain Chambers calling his name.

"Slocum, get out of there! The grass fire's out of control. There's no way we can keep it from moving downhill. Go upslope! Do it now or you'll be burned alive!"

Slocum hesitated. Penks was in the mine, but all around came leaping tongues of flame. They started small, but quickly found new fuel and jumped higher. Slocum saw that he could never outrun the fast-spreading fire by going downhill. Chambers was right. The only escape lay uphill.

"The fire's out of control, Penks. Get out of the mine or you'll be trapped!" Slocum shouted.

"Run, Slocum, run!" shouted Chambers.

"John, do as he says. Please!" came Cara's shrill voice. "Go uphill!"

Slocum made his decision. He backed from the mine, then scrambled up the rocky slope to the left of the mine. His boots dug into the shale and made progress slow, but the incentive of fire licking at his back gave him speed he had never known he possessed. Slocum finally reached a level spot fifty feet above the mouth of the mine and looked back.

The grass fire had reached the mouth of the mine. Smoke billowed in, then Slocum saw a sudden change. Smoke gushed from the mine. He sucked in his breath. The dry timbers had caught fire. Under him Slocum felt the shifting of rock and heard the grinding, groaning sounds as support timbers gave way inside the mine.

Smoke was replaced with dust and debris as the mine collapsed, trapping Arly Penks inside.

Slocum couldn't be sure, but he thought he heard distant screams of agony. He trudged along the edge of the blazing fire and circled back to where Doc Hanley tended Cara and several of the volunteer firemen who had ventured too close to the fire and had received burns.

"Land o' Goshen, Slocum, get yourself over here. You're in worse shape than any of these fine folks," Hanley barked when he saw Slocum's condition.

Slocum sank to the ground next to Cara and let the doctor work his magic on his blistered back and cut arms and a dozen other minor injuries Slocum was barely aware of receiving. Doc Hanley covered Slocum with lime water, linseed oil, and lint, making a temporary but effective dressing for his burns.

"John?" Cara's expression was a mixture of fear and hope. He knew how she must feel, traveling across a continent to find a lost brother, only to have him try to murder her. Confusion had to grip her at every turn. Did she wish for Arly Penk's death or his survival?

"He went into the mine," Slocum said. "It collapsed."

"What's that?" Doc Hanley looked around. "Somebody went into that old mine?"

Slocum only nodded.

"There's no safety shaft out of it. That was one reason it was abandoned," Hanley said. He shook his head in dejection. "The other was that nobody ever found more than a nickel's worth of silver in it after more than a year of digging." He finished the bandage across Slocum's back and stepped away to admire his handiwork.

"Feels better. Thanks, Doc," Slocum said.

"Durned good work, if I do say so myself. Now, who was it in the mine? Digging him out is going to be the work of a week or longer."

Slocum glanced at Cara. She was pale but composed. She spoke before Slocum could respond.

"That's all right, doctor," Cara Penks said. "Mr. Slocum didn't mean anyone was in the mine. It was just possible that someone might have run into it for shelter. I am sure he was wrong."

Hanley snorted and went to work on others who had been injured fighting the fire. Slocum waited for Cara to speak again.

"Well, John, what should I have said? Dig it up? My brother's buried, and he tried to kill me?"

"He'll have a nice funeral service he doesn't deserve. This time, we know where the body is," Slocum said.

"Good riddance," she said with sudden venom. "He was no real brother. He was no real son to my father." She shivered in spite of the heat from the fire. Slocum reached out and took her hand.

"We've got a passel of money to spend, the two of us," Slocum said. "The owners of the Croaking Frog offered fifty thousand dollars for the silver Jackass Mine. How do you think we should start getting rid of that money?" Their eyes locked and a small smile crept onto the lovely raven-haired woman's lips.

"First of all, we ought to find a good bathhouse and get

cleaned up. Then something to eat. Hmm, what then?'' Her blue eyes twinkled with real merriment. Slocum was happy to see her change in mood.

"A hotel," he suggested. "We need to catch up on sleep."

"And more," Cara said, holding her arm out for Slocum to take. Together they made their way through the volunteer firemen from Monumental Engine Company No. 6, down the slope from Gold Hill, and back into Virginia City.

If you enjoyed this book, subscribe now and get...

TWO FREE

A $7.00 VALUE–

A special offer for people who enjoy reading the best Westerns published today.

WESTERNS!

NO OBLIGATION

Mail the coupon below

To start your subscription and receive 2 FREE WESTERNS, fill out the coupon below and mail it today. We'll send your first shipment which includes 2 FREE BOOKS as soon as we receive it.

- -